H. C. Dutt

Writings, Spiritual, Moral and Poetic

H. C. Dutt

Writings, Spiritual, Moral and Poetic

ISBN/EAN: 9783337334376

Printed in Europe, USA, Canada, Australia, Japan

Cover: Foto ©Andreas Hilbeck / pixelio.de

More available books at **www.hansebooks.com**

WRITINGS,

SPIRITUAL, MORAL AND POETIC.

BY

H. C. DUTT.

"Our senses can grasp nothing that is in extreme. Too much noise deafens us; too great light blinds us; too great a distance or too much proximity equally prevents us from being able to see; too long and too short a discourse obscures our knowledge of a subject; too much of truth stuns us."

PASCAL.

"Song is but the eloquence of truth."—CAMPBELL.

Calcutta:

PRINTED BY P. S. D'ROZARIO AND CO., 12, WATERLOO STREET,

1878.

PREFACE.

ADDISON has remarked " that a reader seldom peruses a book with pleasure till he knows whether the writer of it be a black or a fair man, of a mild or choleric disposition, married or a bachelor," and so forth. It had better be stated then, by way of preface, that the author of this book is a Bengali Convert, educated at the old Hindu College. Amid disadvantages from sickness, he has had some time to devote to literary occupations. He has a family, several children, all from the Old Stock of Hinduism, but who have by God's blessing escaped its trammels and are with him in the faith to which he has been called.

RAMBAGAN COTTAGE ;

172, *Manicktolla Street.*

INDEX.

DISCOURSES, &c.

POEMS.—RELIGIOUS.

POEMS.—INDIAN.

POEMS.—MISCELLANEOUS.

DISCOURSES,
&c.

The Wisdom of Babedom.

At that time Jesus answered and said, I thank thee O Father, Lord of heaven and earth, because thou hast hid these things from the wise and prudent, and hast revealed them unto babes. Even so Father for so it seemed good in thy sight.—MATTHEW 11. (25-26.)

THE divine origin of Christianity is the most remarkable feature which distinguishes it from all other religions in the world. Comparing it with Vedantism and Puranism, the monotheistic and polytheistic religions of India, or with the religions of ancient Greece, Rome or Egypt, this difference is clearly discernible. In the one case it is a subjective effort of the human mind, in the other an objective reality—in the one case man has attempted to trace God in his handiwork or to invent divinities for homage and adoration, in the other God has spoken through the prophets, through Christ, and through His Spirit—in the one case there has been "working from below upwards," in the other light has proceeded from above—at first a beautiful dawn, then brighter radiance and meridian splendour! Nor have visible manifestations of the Almightiness of God been wanting. Olympus and its inhabitants, Kailasa and its divinities, sink into utter nothingness before the glories of Zion. Even where men have been able to feel after God by efforts or processes of intellect, the light has served only to make "darkness visible." The book of Nature is a book of hieroglyphics. It is symbolical of higher and purer things in the background. Observe again the mystery of life. Its cabalistic characters cannot be deciphered, except by light from on high. What am I? why created? whither destined? Whence these joys and sorrows, hopes, aspirations, longings? Apply the lamp of Divine Truth to the subject, and it breaks and dissolves into a thousand variegated flowers fit only for the lawns and groves of Paradise.

The passage quoted above shows most forcibly our Lord's estimate of worldly wisdom, worldly foresight, in short, of worldly culture. The same idea under a somewhat different modification is also traceable in St. Paul's Epistle to the Corinthians. "For it is written I will destroy the wisdom of the wise and will bring to nothing the understanding of the prudent. Where is the wise? Where is the scribe? Where is the disputer of this world? For after that in the wisdom of God, the world by wisdom knew not God, it pleased God by the foolishness of preaching to save them that believe." It will thus be seen that the Bible estimate of human culture is exceedingly low. Divine and miraculous in its origin it repudiates all but divine and miraculous agencies in the conversion of souls. There is no doubt that the world is striving for perfection, not by a spiritual regeneration from on high but by intellectual culture and aggrandisement, which is essentially only a repetition of the principle announced by the Serpent in Paradise—Man is to attain of himself without God's special help and favor, to the highest knowledge and thereby to equality with God. This principle found its 'colossal manifestation' in the tower of Babel, and is exemplified in the heathen nations of antiquity, in their sculptures, their paintings, their philosophy and poetry, when compared with the Jews. Herein also consists the great error of our times that culture or education is thought to be the highest thing, the panacea for all evils, and is looked upon as a substitute for divine grace, for renovation by the Spirit of the living God.

Let us, therefore, in an humble and childlike spirit continue to ask of God for a fuller appreciation of His revealed will, to say "open Thou our eyes and we shall behold wondrous things out of Thy law." The life in God forms no part of the present world-course. "The fashion of this world passeth away." Not that culture if properly directed cannot be made subservient to the glory of God and good of man, not that education is to be neglected or despised, not that civilization *per se* is anything wicked or sinful, but they are not what the world makes them to be—our highest good, or even the vehicles or media of that highest good. This will be abundantly evident from our Lord's words quoted as text.

Among the apostles, Paul was the only one who could lay claim to culture or erudition. A reader of the Greek drama and practised in the mental gymnastics which could then be learnt only within the circle of Greek philosophy, dialectics and rhetoric, and having also a knowledge of sculpture and painting, he certainly was different from the other Galilean teachers but for the unity and simplicity in Christ, which made them all one, and for which he counted all other things "as dung." We know also that his *erudition* had nothing to do with his *conversion*, which was by special miraculous means. So that the truth enunciated holds good. Would it not be a blessed day if the world contained more men like the primitive apostles, the poor unlearned fishermen of Galilee?

The renovation of the earth will never be brought about by any mere human means, nor can we say except from Holy writ, what convulsions and throes will attend the disruption of the old, and the inauguration of the new order of things. Looking into the pages of history we see successive civilizations rise, culminate, and sink into everlasting gloom. Assyria, Nineveh, Babylon, Egypt, Greece, and Rome had each its boasted day of natural progress, but like the lost Pleiads are now no more. The last was the mistress of the then known world. The Roman eagle was the terror of the nations. Wherever it alighted and clapped its wings, it conquered. But alas! it dropped its feathers and lost the brightness of its piercing eyes, and was trampled upon by barbarian hordes. India too had its days of intellectual excellence. The beauty of its ancient literature, the depth and subtlety of its ancient philosophy are abundant evidence of this fact. Humanity unaided by a renovating process from on high must needs degenerate and decline. As it is with individual souls, so is it with nations. The true preservative is the grace of God, the simplicity as it is in Christ Jesus.

There is but one path then to the acquisition of divine

truth, to stability, glory, immortality. "If any man will become wise let him become a fool." To unlearn all wisdom is the highest wisdom. To those who pride themselves upon their knowledge and reason, I would say that you must come down from the pedestal of self-righteousness upon which you have placed yourselves and must relinquish the self-sufficiency of your own ways. You must enter in by the same gate as the unlearned, the simple, and the ignorant. You must listen with reverent attention to the inspired Oracles of God. You must sit at the feet of Jesus and learn. And surely it is no humiliation to learn from Him who is the Lord of Glory and Chief among ten thousand ! It requires only a child-like spirit to be able to discern the depth and simplicity of these words of Scripture, " God hath chosen the foolish things of the world to confound the wise, and God hath chosen the weak things of the world to confound the things which are mighty, and base things of the world and things which are despised, yea, and things which are not to bring to nought things that are : that no flesh should glory in his presence."

Lastly, let us for a few moments direct our attention to that beautiful scene in the temple at Jerusalem described by St. Matthew, where, when the chief priests and scribes saw the miracles wrought by the great Healer and heard the children crying out "Hosanna to the son of David," they were enraged. Their superior culture and erudition could not bear it. With what benignity are they put to shame ! When asked in derision " Hearest thou what the children say," he replies out of the writings of the same David whom they acknowledge as prophet and king !—"yea, have ye never read, out of the mouth of babes and sucklings thou hast perfected praise." May we now and at all times be able to join in that infant chorus first raised in the temple at Jerusalem :

"Hosanna to the living Lord,
Hosanna to the Incarnate word ;
To Christ, Creator, Saviour, King,
Let earth, let Heaven Hosanna sing.
        Hosanna ! Lord ! Hosanna in the highest !

Hosanna ! Lord ! Thine angels cry,
Hosanna ! Lord ! Thy saints reply ;
Above, beneath us, and around,
The dead and living swell the sound.
        Hosanna !Lord ! Hosanna in the highest !

So in the last and dreadful day,
When earth and heaven shall melt away ;
Thy flock redeemed from sinful stain,
Shall swell the sound of praise again.
        Hosanna ! Lord ! Hosanna in the highest !"

Resurrection.

It is sown a natural ; it is raised a spiritual body.—

1 Cor. 15. (44.)

THERE are innumerable hidden forces in Nature about which we understand little or nothing.   We know of the existence of such forces, we daily witness their operations, we characterise them by distinguishing names, but the *why* and *wherefore* is and will perhaps ever remain a mystery.   The attractions of cohesion and gravitation, the polarity of the needle and the law of germination are instances of this. Little do we know when out on our summer-evening's stroll *why* the particles of earth under our feet cohere and bear us up. Little do youths engaged in pleasant pastime know *why* the ball flung up high into the air returns to the earth. Little does the mariner know *why* under a beclouded sky and ever roaring waters the small instrument before him is true to the invisible Cynosure. Little does the sower know *why* in a few days the scattered seed springs up into green and tender blades glistening with the dews of heaven. Nature has also its hidden treasures. In this wonder-teeming world the commonest things often yield the richest and noblest results. The silkworm ejects from its bowels materials for costly raiment, the juice of the grape so insignificant in size and so plentiful in the temperate regions affords beverages which have been compared by poets to the nectar of the gods, nay, the chemical constituents of coal are identical with those of the brightest diamond which ever graced a monarch's diadem. All the mineral wealth of the world, the pearls imbedded in the Ocean in their shell-covers, are intrinsically no better than lumps of clod, and do not assume a value till they have passed into man's hand. Nor are the hidden beauties of Nature less remarkable. How captivating is a ray of light passed through a prism. What variety, what richness, what exuberance of coloring! The telescope and the microscope disclose unseen beauties. In the common house-fly what fascinating green and gold, and in that dimly descried track in the skies, the milky way, what a galaxy of stars glowing with heaven's own effulgence. Nature is an Eastern potentate, and has his hidden forces, his hidden treasures, and his hidden seraglio of beauties.

What wonder then if this frail tenement of ours raised out of the dust, and returning to the dust, should contain the germs of an immortal and glorious body to be evolved when the Sun of Righteousness shall arise with healing on its wings. What wonder if God in His infinite wisdom has thought fit to disclose this truth by Revelation from on high and not by the ordinary processes of intellectual generalization. That this has been the case will be manifest from a glance at all other religions. None of the ancient religions speak of the doctrine of the Resurrection of the body. Hinduism, which seems to have been the origin of every other form of superstitious belief, and which in its wide-spread and elaborate ramifications may be compared to the banian of Indian growth, exhibits passages in its sacred books which may be construed as allusions to it, but nowhere except in the Bible is it prominently foreshadowed as a doctrine. In the following passage from the Bhagvat Geeta, or Dialogues between Krishna and Arjun, one of the most esteemed of the sacred books of the Hindus, a faint glimmering of this truth is discernible : " As a man throweth away old garments and putteth on new, even so the soul having quitted its old mortal frame entereth into others which are new. The weapon divideth it not, the fire burneth it not, the water corrupteth it not, the wind drieth it not away, for it is indivisible, inconsumable, incorruptible, and is not to be dried away, it is eternal, universal, permanent, immoveable, it is invisible, inconceivable, and unalterable, therefore believing it to be thus, thou shouldest not grieve, but whether thou believest it of eternal truth and duration, or that it dieth with the body, still thou hast no cause to lament it. Death is certain to all things which are subject to birth and *regeneration to all things which are mortal.*" Again in the Yajur Ved, " The pure enlightened soul assumes a luminous form with no gross body, with no perforation, with no veins or tendons, unblemished, untainted by sin, itself being a ray from the infinite spirit, which knows the past and the future, which pervades all, which existed with no cause but itself, which created all things as they are in ages very remote."

The fanciful doctrine of transmigrations seems to occupy the same place in the Hindu economy of Redemption that Resurrection occupies in the Christian. According to Menu, the slayer of a Brahmin must enter, according to the circumstances of his crime, the body of a dog, a boar, an ass, a camel, a bull, a goat, a sheep, a stag, a bird ; a priest fond of drinking shall migrate into the form of a smaller or larger worm or insect, of a moth, of a fly, or of some ravenous animal. He who steals the gold of a priest, shall pass a thousand times into the bodies of spiders, of snakes, and chameleons, of crocodiles, and other aquatic monsters or of mischievous blood-sucking demons. They who hurt any sentient beings are born cats and other eaters of raw flesh ; they who taste interdicted food, maggots or small flies ; they who steal grain, a rat ; they who steal perfumes, a muskrat ; they who steal fruits, an ape ; and so on. As far as human souls will indulge and wallow in sensuality and forbidden pleasures, so far, according to Menu, will the acuteness of their senses be raised in their future bodies that they may endure analogous pains. This is by no means dissimilar to the opinion of Socrates as represented by Plato. " When the soul soiled and impure quits the body having during its earthly life lived only for sensual things, having been kept

B

fascinated by material things, but having hated and repulsed the invisible and supernatural things, do you think that such a soul will depart entirely pure and free ? By no means ; for penetrated by the material and carrying it with it as a burden, as something earthly and visible, it will be depressed, and again drawn towards the region of visible things, fearing the invisible world and hades."

Spring is the emblem of Resurrection. But the glories of a full-blown spring are not to be seen in this land. They are fleeting and evanescent in the extreme. Our own Kalidasa divides the year into six seasons and not four, as the English poets divide it. Beautiful as is Kalidasa's description of spring, the idea that it is the emblem of Resurrection is entirely absent. The breeze laden with perfumes, moving softly over the flower-enamelled lake, the koil and the bee, the blossoming mangoe-groves are beautifully described, but the hidden meaning of spring does not seem to have been appreciated.

> " But when the blood chills and the years go by,
> As we resemble Autumn more, the more
> We love the Resurrection-time of spring ;
> And spring is now around me. Snow-drops come,
> Sad sweet memorials of a man I loved,
> The crocus gleams along the garden walk,
> And from the tree top sings the speckled thrush ;
> Within the flying sunlights twinkling troops
> Of chaffinches jerk here and there, beneath
> The shrubbery the blackbird runs, then flits
> With chattering cry, and at the ploughman's heel
> Within the red-drawn furrow stalks the rook."

The seed sown in the furrows of God's acre, will one day shoot up into the light and life of an eternal spring.

Another illustrative analogy of the Resurrection—not the less beautiful because it is trite—is to be seen in the butterfly. It is only after the crawling worm has been *entombed* that it rises up into the sunlight of a new and glorified existence. Can any one say by what process the Divine Alchemist out of the dust formed the body of Adam compared to which our present bodies are emphatically vile. Cannot He, out of the wrecks of that Adamic body, form another more glorious than the first, one like unto his own? Is not this, in accordance with all God's dealings with man, viewing it even as a spiritual truth? The most un-promising materials, such as men think fit to be swept away, may in God's hand be converted into the pure gold of the Temple, into jewels of surpassing loveliness. Witness the case of St. Paul and of Mary Magdalene and of hundreds of God's people in ancient and modern times. "Though ye have lien among the pots, ye shall yet be as the wings of a dove covered with silver and her feathers with yellow gold."

And now conceive how vast the number of glorified bodies which shall surround the Great White Throne of the Eternal on the Resurrection-morn, a countless multi-tude out of every tongue and clime and nation. Conceive all the host of heaven, the angels, and arch-angels, the cherubims and seraphims crying holy! holy! holy! Conceive the hyaline pavement which John saw in vision stretching far away into shining distance before the throne of God! Conceive countless golden harps all attuned to sound praises to God and to the Lamb! Behind, before, on every side, in native and reflected blaze, chariots of fire and horses of fire! And then the trump of wondrous melody never heard before, proceeding out of the royal city New Jerusalem, whose light is like unto a stone most precious even like a jasperstone clear as crystal ! And in the midst of all these glories He who by becoming flesh of our flesh and bone of our bone has wrought all this transfiguration, one like unto the Son of Man !

St. Paul.

I am crucified with Christ, nevertheless I live.—GALATIANS 2. (20.)

PERHAPS the substrata which underlie the characters of God's hero and the world's hero are not so dissimilar as people imagine, and the contrast lies only in the motives or springs of action. For about six thousand years the world has been huzzaing every undetected pilferer, every successful cut-throat, and will continue to do so to the end of time. But the brass which the world so admires is transmutable into pure gold by one touch of that substance which alchemists seek in vain and which God gives, but for the asking, in the shape of a ray of heavenly light. Napoleon the Great would still have been great, but in a different sense, if he had enlisted in the ranks of God's soldiery and been faithful. His courage, his education, the force and quickness of his intellect, the devotion of all his energies to his cherished object, his knowledge of human nature, and his power of swaying men according to his will, would all have been turned to the happiest account. His bloody victories would have been victories of faith—instead of leading multitudinous hosts to destruction, he would have led out multitudes of souls to life everlasting ; instead of plans to subjugate the nations of Europe, he would have planned attacks against the powers of darkness ; instead of waging war with humanity, he would have waged war with the evils which besiege it, with its errors, its follies, and its crimes. Not with a sword of steel, but with a sword forged in the armoury of heaven would he have fought his battles ; not an earthly diadem but for him would have been laid up " a crown of glory." And when the shadows of death were closing around him, not a vision of sublunary grandeur as betrayed in the words " têté d'armée," but a sure hope of an eternal morning, and a name registered among the noble army of martyrs ! O soldier of Christ ! watch well the motives and springs of action : for out of these are the issues of life. What similarity and contrast in the characters of Napoleon surnamed "great," and Paul which signifies " little" !

It would be useless to attempt anything like an essay on the life and writings of St. Paul within the limits which we have assigned to each of these discourses. So rich in doctrine the latter, and so various and interesting the incidents in the former that volumes would not suffice, supposing we had the requisite ability. Merging the abstract into the concrete, we shall here present only a few passages from the life of the man whom we have styled " God's hero."

Paul educated at the feet of Gamaliel, Paul the Pharisee, Paul the Persecutor, was indeed different from Paul the converted, Paul the man of faith, and Paul who wrote, " I am crucified with Christ, nevertheless I live." Frail in body he seems always to have been, but the fiery spirit, working out its way in a wrong channel, was arrested by grace and brought to the feet of the Saviour. By profession he was a tent-maker. Raphael has painted him weak and infirm, and Luther thought him "a poor, lean, little man like master Philip" (Melancthon). Gamaliel's teaching, however, was not the limit of Paul's education. His native town Tarsus was celebrated for its zeal for philosophy and other branches of knowledge, and here he seems to have diligently studied the Greek poets and philosophers. He inherited from his father the privileges of a Roman citizen, and while engaged in such studies, and while the prophet's cry was being echoed and re-echoed in the surrounding gloom, "Watchman what of the night?" the morning had already broken over the walls of the temple at Jerusalem. From his youth he seems to have been a lover of Nature, and the fruitful plains at the foot of the Taurus, and the jessamine and oleander shrubs 'on the banks of the Cydnus must to him have been delights. But the hidden meaning of Nature he had yet to see through "the true light."

"Touching the righteouness which is in the law blameless." To keep the faith (not knowing at the time what faith is) and induce others to do so till Messiah should appear (that day of Israel's triumph over all her enemies) was the desperate struggle of his mind. A work, a legal virtue, the due respect and literal observance of all God-appointed institutions and ordinances, circumcision, the passover, the reading of the law and the prophets—these were then his ideas of faith. But the time was coming when they were to be swept away for ever, as filthy rags, making room for "the righteousness of God in Christ."

The scene, at the murder of the proto-martyr Stephen,

is one of the most remarkable in that great life-drama, so full of incidents and adventure. It is described first in the Acts, and the history of Paul unfolds itself from that starting point, partly from the accounts given of him by Luke, but principally from his own speeches and epistles. The words " the witnesses laid down their clothes at a young man's feet whose name was Saul," and " Saul was consenting unto his death," are sufficient to indicate to the careful discerner of character that the young zealot was the heart and soul of the awful business. The celebrated Spanish painter Vicente Joannes has represented Paul as walking at the martyr's side, lost in profound meditation, in striking contrast with the wild rabble—fervent devotion is seen on his face, and on his brow gleams a ray of light from Stephen's face, which ray he is attempting strenuously to ward off. This is just before the martyrdom scene, when certain of the synagogue, which is called the synagogue of the Libertines and Cyrenians and Alexandrians, set up false witnesses against Stephen, who said, " this man ceaseth not to speak blasphemous words against this holy place and the Law, and all that looked steadfastly on him, saw his face as it had been the face of an angel."

High noon on the plains of Damascus. Naked and slaty rocks bounded the horizon. The domes and minarets of the sacred city rose from amid super-abounding vegetation, nature revelling in beautiful luxuriance, the tasseled garniture of eastern climes. The palm and the cypress, the orange and the citron, drooped in the noon-day heat, and a rich perfume exhaled from beds of flowers. The streamlets laughed in the sunlight. But neither the beauty of the scene, nor the glad sunlight could dispel the gloom which sat on the brow and in the heart of the horseman, who, with his retinue, was approaching the city. God had his own purposes. The "chosen vessel" would attract light from heaven. Down, down he falls bewildered and stunned. The Light, the Lord Jesus, brighter than the sun at noonday, has shined into his heart, has blinded his eyes so set on destruction, has made Paul 'breathing out threatening and slaughter' into the obedient and willing slave of the Lord Jesus. "Paul—Paul, why persecutest thou Me!" Thus, indeed, did the Lord honour His church, making it one with Himself in time and eternity.

Next, let us see Paul 'in bonds'—in bonds but no bondman, for Christ had made him *free.* Slave to God and not to man. "My yoke is easy and My burden is light." Rejoicing in his chains in so far as they furnished occasion to preach 'Christ crucified,' fearless alike of the pains and penalties which his conduct might entail, filled with a sanctified fervor and joy, the uncompromising spirit of the Benjamite stirred up within him in the cause of his Lord and Master, he had occasion to give vent at Cæsarea, to those outbursts of holy eloquence which will ever remain unrivalled. The loving kindness of that Master he had signally experienced. Brought out of the darkness of the Law into the full effulgence of Gospel-light in a miraculous manner, and feeling that God is Love and God is Light, he was indeed 'a spectacle unto angels and to men' in strange contrast to the figures which surrounded him, his enemies, accusers, and judges, to the high priest Ananias who directed the mob to smite him on the mouth, to Claudius Lysias, the chief captain with a dash of boldness, but yet with a due respect for constituted authority, to the orator Tertullus with his address and volubility, to the mercenary Felix and his petted Drusilla, to the dignified Festus, to Herod Agrippa, the last Jewish King in his robes of royalty and to the fascinating but immoral Bernice. Before a brilliant assembly Paul closed his series of apostolic defences. "Having, therefore, obtained help of God, I continue unto this day witnessing both to small and great, saying none other things than those which the prophets and Moses did say should come, that Christ should suffer, and that He should be the first that should rise from the dead, and should shew light unto the people and to the gentiles." Thus did he again proclaim the crucified Jesus, as the "light of the gentiles"! Interrupted by Festus with the half sarcastic and half respectful remark " Paul thou art beside thyself, much learning doth make thee mad," he dexterously parries the thrust by an appeal to the Judaism of King Herod, to the Law and to the testimony of the prophets. And when the King after listening with rapt attention says, "Almost thou persuadest me to be a Christian," the well-springs of love in Paul's heart bubble up and he pronounces a benediction on all present with the concluding words "except these bonds"!

About Paul's voyage to Italy and the events which followed, we have no room to speak. How, though a prisoner, he tamed a mutinous crew, how the wind called Euroclydon arose baffling the skill of all on board, how he turned sailor, how he stepped forth amid the despairing and cheered them with the assurance of safety which the angel of God had given unto him, how the shipwrecked party came to know their deliverer as one who had ' power to tread on serpents,' how he entered Rome and addressed some beautiful epistles from that place, must all remain untold. Sufficient has been said to shew what a man, what a hero, what a Christian, he was. To live unto Christ in all things was his glory, and to present every man perfect in Christ Jesus, the aim of his renewed life. Such was the man who in weariness and painfulness, in perils of robbers, in perils of waters, in perils of wild beasts, in stripes and in imprisonment, had something to uphold him which no one could take away. Such was St. Paul, true son of Benjamin, honor of Israel, who was "all things unto all men"!

And now may God make each soldier of Christ like unto this Hebrew of Hebrews, granting him an equal measure of faith and hope and love!

Ruth.

And Orpah kissed her mother-in-law, but Ruth clave unto her.—
RUTH 1. (14.)

O DEAR delectable Ruth! Can we ever forget thee? Thirty centuries and more have elapsed since thou gleanedst on the fields near Bethlehem-judah in the beginning of barley-harvest, and yet thy love and thy beauty exercise their fascinating influence on all who read thy story, are the delight of the old and the young, the model for women, and the theme and inspiration of the poet !

> " She stood breast-high amid the corn,
> Clasped by the golden light of morn,
> Like the sweet-heart of the sun
> Who many a glowing kiss had won.
>
> On her cheek, an autumn flush
> Deeply ripened ;—such a blush
> In the midst of brown was born,
> Like red poppies grown with corn.
>
> Round her eyes her tresses fell,
> Which were blackest, none could tell,
> But long lashes veil'd a light
> That had else been all too bright.
>
> Thus she stood amid the stooks
> Praising God with sweetest looks."

The history of Ruth, the Moabitess, is not only delightful reading, but is full of consoling edification. Here we have a foreshadowing of the " Old Old story" in all its simplicity and beauty, not in a parable, fable, myth, or allegory, but in the lives of human beings. The incidents are not only true to nature, true to Revelation, but are true as facts, and as such possess an additional interest and value. We find here those peculiar sensibilities, that tenderness and that affectionate self-devotion which characterise woman in the East, and which the education and the independence so highly extolled in our day seem to be wearing off. We find how piety, duty, and love may overcome trials and difficulties, which but for them would appear insuperable. We find how happiness flows from a reliance on God even under the most adverse circumstances. We find how, having wandered away, a person may yet return to God who is ever ready to welcome and to save. We find the supreme importance of casting in our lot with God's people. We find how seeking the kingdom of God and His Righteousness all other things are added unto us. We find an exemplification in Ruth herself of what has been so artistically described by Milton "pure-eyed faith, white-handed hope, and the unblemished form of chastity." We find the supermundane or spiritual aspect of the marriage-tie. We find how after weeping which endureth for the night, joy cometh in the morning! All these and much more we find in the Book of Ruth, and we consider it a pleasure rather than a task to trace this history, as it unfolds itself in its beautifully diversified colors.

Behold that group of wandering Israelites! From whither are they wandering and whereto bound? It is from Bethlehem they are wandering; Bethlehem "the house of bread," Bethlehem within whose gates was a pellucid spring of refreshing waters; Bethlehem around which were concentered the Jew's most devout associations; Bethlehem the promised birth-place of the Messiah; Bethlehem the glorious was this discontented family deserting, because there was a famine in the land. It was a hasty, foolish wandering after all. Whither are they going? To the land of Moab, a land of idolatry and crime which has "fulness of bread like that in Sodom." The man's name was Elimelech (God my king), the woman's name Naomi (Pleasant), and the names of the two sons Mahlon and Chilion. Alas! that this family should be so ill-judged as to make the exchange, an exchange of the spiritual for the carnal, an exchange the full significance of which can only be understood by contemplating the Moab within and around us, "the lust of the flesh, and the lust of the eye, and the pride of life."

A few short years and circumstances are sadly changed. Elimelech, Mahlon, and Chilion are now no more, and Naomi, with two widowed daughters-in-law Orpah and Ruth, Moabitesses, feels her desolation. She begins to think about and afterwards to long for home. It almost reminds one of the prodigal's longing for his father's house in the parable which has been called the gospel of the Gospels (Evangelium in Evangelio.) Her afflictions have been so overwhelming and so bitter that she can hardly stand them. "Call me not Naomi (pleasant) she said, but call me Mara (bitter), for the Almighty hath dealt very bitterly with me." Yes, poor Naomi seems to have forgotten that the fruits of our wandering away from God are bitter indeed ! But observe her tender solicitude for her widowed daughters-in-law even then. " And Naomi said unto her daughters-in-law, Go, return each to her mother's house : the Lord deal kindly with you as ye have dealt with the dead and with me." But whether this apparent discouragement was the language of the innermost core of her soul seems very doubtful. Orpah kissed her mother-in-law, but Ruth clave unto her ; clave unto her to go forward to the land of Israel, " for thy people," she said, " shall be my people, and thy God my God."

It is the beginning of barley harvest. The cerulean aspect of the sky bespeaks unutterable peace, and stretching far to the hill-side of Judea are the cornfields separated by landmarks, rippling in light and shade like a golden sea. Everything is astir. The voice of the reapers is heard. The bleating of sheep and the lowing of cattle come softly vibrating in the mellow morning air. The kite and the hawk are wheeling overhead, the swallow is darting in fitful eddies, and here and there a solitary lapwing is lazily travelling along sounding its oft-repeated note pee-wit! pee-wit! At this season of the year when the universal frame of nature is blessed by God's bountiful hand, and earth seems linked to heaven as in a bridal-knot, all hearts seem happy. To the Jewish people it was a season of peculiar significance, for it bespoke of the feast of Tabernacles or ingathering commemorative of the sojourn of Israel in the desert, that feast which is enjoined to be celebrated by dwelling in booths seven days, and by "the boughs of goodly trees, branches of palm-trees, and the boughs of thick trees, and willows of the brook, and by rejoicing before the Lord God."—Lev. 23, (40.) The sympathizing heart of poor, stricken Ruth partook in some measure of the general feeling of the people whom she had espoused and adopted. "And Naomi had a kinsman of her husband, a mighty man of wealth of the family of Elimelech, and his name was Boaz. And Ruth, the Moabitess, said unto Naomi, "let me now go to the field and glean ears of corn after him in whose sight I shall find grace." And she said unto her, "go my daughter." Thus then was the dark-eyed Ruth in the field of Boaz, in all the loveliness of her youthful charms, in all the security of conscious virtue, toiling away for a mother's support and comfort. And when Boaz came to visit his well ordered fields, nothing seemed to him more beautiful than the conduct of Ruth. And Boaz answered and said unto her, "It hath been fully showed me, all that thou hast done unto thy mother-in-law since the death of thine husband ; and how thou hast left thy father and thy mother, and the land of thy nativity, and hast come unto a people which thou knewest not heretofore. The Lord recompense thy work, and a full reward be given thee of the Lord God of Israel under whose wings thou art come to trust." How this approval grew up into intimacy and admiration, how Ruth in meek humility lay at the feet of her kinsman, how she kept company with the maidens of Boaz and not with the young men, "whether poor or rich," and details of this description are related with that divine simplicity which pervades the pages of this book. But perhaps the most instructive point at the close of the history is the *redemption* proposed and accomplished by Boaz. "Then went Boaz and sat him down there : and behold the kinsman of whom Boaz spake came by, unto whom he said, Ho, such-a-one, turn aside, sit down here. And he turned aside, and sat down. And he took ten men of the elders of the city, and said, sit down here. And they sat down. And he said unto the kinsman, Naomi that is come again out of the country of Moab, selleth a parcel of land which was our brother Elimelech's, and I thought to advertise thee saying buy it before the inhabitants and before the elders of my people. If thou wilt redeem it, redeem it ; but if thou wilt not redeem it, then tell me that L may know ; for there is none to redeem it besides thee, and I am after thee." Now the redemption here proposed was by marrying a deceased brother's wife, and though perfectly in accordance with the Jewish law, this is the first and last notable instance of it mentioned in Scripture : the kinsman having refused, Boaz stepped in, and the marriage was accomplished. "And all the people that were in the gate, and the elders said we are witnesses.

The Lord make the woman that is come unto thine house like Rachel and like Leah, which two did build the house of Israel; and do thou worthily in Ephratah and be famous in Bethlehem." Reader, are you bereaved? Are you poor? Are you cast down? You *have* a rich kinsman who hath redeemed you. Go to Him and lie at his feet, and you will have richer consolation than ever cometh from the power of man!

Jonah.

So Jonah arose and went unto Nineveh.—Jonah 3. (3.)

" OD arbaim yom venineveh nehpācheth," " yet forty days and Nineveh overthrown."—Such was the cry which proceeded from the prophet clad in hairy garments, breaking the stillness of the morning sky as it hung monotonously over the great city Nineveh, sixty miles in extent, with its palaces, gardens and temples, with its statues of great winged bulls and lions with human heads. The debauchee was roused by it, as he was courting the sleep which he had repelled during the night, the babe clung closer to the breast of its young mother, merchants, shop-keepers, artificers, gazed with wonder mingled with awe, and as he passed through the fortifications and the broad gates, the eyes of

the sentinels " clothed in blue" were rivetted towards him.
He who had before fled from the presence of the Lord, now
arose and went at His bidding with the cry, " yet forty days
and Nineveh overthrown." The effect of the preaching was
instantaneous. Nineveh turned unto God. The king of
Nineveh arose from his throne and girded himself with sack-
cloth, and sat on ashes and proclaimed a solemn fast. The
whole city cried mightily, and God's anger was stayed.

But what of Jonah? He had signal experiences of the
Divine mercy when shipping at the one Israelitish port of
Joppa, the sea boiled under him like a seething cauldron,
and the Tyrian sailors cast him overboard, and one of the
monsters of the deep swallowed him up. He had felt the
folly of any attempt to flee from God. He had been converted, yet his human nature gets the mastery over him.
Like the elder brother in the parable, who could not bear seeing the table spread out for the prodigal and music and
dancing, he is in a pet. He would rather see " more than
six-score thousand persons, that cannot discern between their
right hand and their left," destroyed forthwith, than that his
denunciation should remain unrealized. God gently re-
monstrates with him (as the father did with his elder son).
" Doest thou well to be angry"? Yes, poor Jonah himself
rescued from the terrors of the deep, he who had sung " I
went down to the bottoms of the mountains ; the earth with
her bars was about me for ever. Yet hast thou brought up
my life from corruption O Lord my God," he who had
prayed one of the most remarkable prayers recorded in holy
writ, had yet to learn about the height and depth, the
length and breadth of God's love and mercy for his sinful
creatures. Thus is the innate selfishness of the best of men

D

contrasted with the inexclusive, all-embracing character of
that love. The lesson is conveyed to him in a very noble
and pleasing form worthy of the great God from whom it
came, a divine application of the *argumentum ad hominem.*
Behold him once more then, in his booth on the east side
of the city, overshadowed by the broad leaves of a beautiful
plant, the Palma Christi. The sudden springing up of this
verdant bower seemed to have exercised a softening, soothing
influence on his irritated mind. But the canker at the root,
like the canker of selfishness in his own heart, soon made it
nought. The sun and the vehement east wind beat upon his
head, and he wished in himself to die. Then was put forward God's *argumentum ad hominem.* " And God said to
Jonah, doest thou well to be angry for the gourd? And he
said, I do well to be angry even unto death. Then said the
Lord, thou hast had pity on the gourd for the which thou
hast not laboured, neither madest it grow ; which came up in
a night and perished in a night, and should not I spare
Nineveh that great city"?

These four short chapters of Jonah are at once pure,
simple, and edifying. It is poetry in prose order. Every
phrase is vivid, graphic, well-chosen. The picture or set of
pictures is highly colored. There is no daub but everything
in proper tone, order, and combination. The prophet hast-
ing down from the hills of Galilee to flee from God,
the embarkation, the storm, the great city Nineveh most
magnificent of all the capitals of the ancient world, and last
of all the rustic booth overshadowed by the broad leaves and
stellated flowers of the Palma Christi, are subjects for the
painter's highest skill. But what strikes us as most beautiful and sublime is Jonah's song of thanksgiving. There is

a depth, a spiritual richness about it, to which we can scarcely find a parallel. Some passages of the Book of Job, some of the psalms of David, and the song of Hannah come up to but are not to our thinking superior to it.

The great lesson to be gathered from the Book of Jonah is the distinct claim of the Gentile world on the justice and mercy of God, and its recognition by God.

We have already stated that we are no sectarian, and that we should be happy if we could but cast in our lot with the people of God in whichever branch of the visible Church they may be found. We have no sympathy with those who would send unbaptized infants to perdition, or entertain unmeaning and superstitious reverence for the priest. We go further. We sympathise so far as we are able, though we do not, agree with those who hold that all the Gentile nations to whom Christ has not been preached, the ancient Hindus, Romans, Greeks, Persians, may have an opportunity of turning to God.

The character of Jonah is to all to appearance self-contradictory. Its specialty renders it most interesting. He was of Gath-hepher, a town of Galilee, and is mentioned in the 2nd book of Kings (14. 23). " In the fifteenth year of Amaziah the son of Joash king of Judah, Jeroboam the son of Joash king of Israel began to reign in Samaria, and reigned forty and one years. And he did that which was evil in the sight of the Lord ; he departed not from all the sins of Jeroboam, the son of Nebat, who made Israel to sin. He restored the coast of Israel from the entering of Hamath unto the sea of the plain according to the word of the Lord God of Israel, which he spake by the hand of his servant Jonah, the son of Amittai, the prophet which was of Gath-hepher. For the Lord saw the affliction of Israel that it was very bitter : for there was not any shut up, nor any left, nor any helper for Israel." The functions of the prophetic office had thus been exercised by him in his own country and among his own people before he was commissioned to preach repentance to Nineveh. The influence of the Jewish people over other nations, (the Egyptians, the Tyrians, the Babylonians, the Assyrians for example) was very marked in ancient times, and will be so in the latter times, but in a far more effective and salutary way. Israel shall yet be to other nations what Jonah, the son of Amittai, was to the Ninevites. When Israel glorifies God and is again glorified by its God, light will radiate from it and lighten the Gentiles.

And lastly what an exemplification have we here of the goodness and mercy of God, what a practical illustration of the words of the prophet Joel, " He is gracious and merciful, slow to anger and of great kindness, and repenteth Him of the evil." Repenteth Him of the evil! The love of the most indulgent human father cannot in any way bear comparison with the love of God. And when we consider that God who is our Father is also the mightiest potentate, the intrinsic value of this love is heightened a hundredfold. For where there is a combination of the royal and paternal functions, such love can only flow to us-ward after the requirements of His eternal laws have been fully satisfied.

Flowers.

Consider the lilies of the field how they grow; they toil not, neither do they spin.—MATTHEW 6. (28.)

WORDS of instruction, consolation, and hope worthy of the great Master from whose lips they fell! Weigh them in golden scales with the sublimated essence of all poetry, and they shall not be found wanting. The Author of nature is also the lover of nature, a love so tender and so pure as to flutter back from the unseemly gaze of the work-day world. Therefore the more closely we approximate to the similitude of Him, the more intensely the love of nature will be developed in our souls. And this is what may be expected. The beauties of creation were for the delight of man. Those summer sunset clouds which lie entangled among the bars of yon lofty Casuarinas, that green upland slowly commingling with the blue of the embracing horizon, the flowers which skirt our path, retain traces of the beauty of Paradise. Look only to the coloring of flowers, something more exquisite than ever turned out from dyer's vat or painter's brush, and say whether they are wholly of the grossness of earth. Every mood of the mind has there its fitting exponent. Are you gay? Are you meditative? Are you sad? Are you in mourning? Bring flowers to suit each varying mood:

" Bring the rathe primrose that forsaken dies,
The tufted crow-toe, and pale jessamine,
The white pink, and the pansy freak'd with jet,
The glowing violet,
The musk-rose, and the well-attired wood-bine,
With cowslips wan that hang the pensive head."

I have often thought, though it is nothing more than an idle conceit, that flowers are the embroidery-work of the angels. As every flower is emblematic of some affection or quality, the rose of love, the lily of majesty, the jasmine of amiableness, and so forth, they may also be compared to the hieroglyphics of angelic language.

But it is not of the flowers of England or of India that we shall now speak. We all know that both the mother-country and its foster-daughter are decked with some of Flora's richest treasures. The lotus of India is in itself a host. Yet leaving all, we shall endeavour to trace the beautiful significance of the words quoted as text.

Dr. Thomson in his work "The Land and the Book" believes that by the word "lilies" the Huleh lily is meant, "it is very large, and the three inner petals meet above and form a gorgeous canopy, such as art never approached, and king never sat under even in his utmost glory. And when I met this incomparable flower in all its loveliness among the oak woods around the northern base of Tabor and on the hills of Nazareth, where our Lord spent His youth, I felt assured, that it was this to which He referred." Others however are inclined to think that the word "lilies" is decidedly synechdochical, and means all wild flowers. We are inclined to the latter view, as "the lilies" here seem to form part of the grass of the field 'which to-day is and to-morrow is cast into the oven' alluded to immediately after. The spiritual application of the example is striking. As the beauty of the flower is unfolded from within, so from within, by a process of evolution, are Christian graces developed in the man; again the humblest of God's handiwork is superior to the proudest effort of man for his own glory; and lastly, there is the teaching that to take anxious thought for the things of the world, for food and raiment, in preference to reliance on the Great Giver is, after all, foolishness. Here and everywhere in Holy Scripture the dignity of man as lord of creation is distinctly upheld. It is this dignity which belonged to him when God Almighty first planted a garden, and which shall yet be his in its original form, when the wilderness of this world shall rejoice and blossom as the rose.

What a fitting analogy have we in flowers to the silent growth of the soul unto God! If there is any fact fully established, it is this : that in the majority of cases the growth of the soul in grace is a very slow process. As petal after petal slowly opens, fed by the refreshing dews of Hermon, the odour of sanctity has a wider range. " In quietness and in confidence shall be your strength." Many a soul has issued from the silence of the cell or the closet or retired leisure redolent of the love of God and man. We can thus account why poets, whom I rank next to apostles and prophets, have a partiality for a life of comparative isolation and inactivity. Not that such a life is absolutely required, for even among throngs of people and amid the busiest concerns of life, we might so hedge in our souls, as to be out of the influence of noxious exhalations and open to the light of heaven, yet it is a fact that poets have a predilection for it.

Hence Milton

> And add to these retired Leisure,
> That in trim gardens takes his pleasure.

And Cowley

> Oh ! fountains ! when in yon shall I
> Myself, eased of unpeaceful thoughts espy ?
> Oh fields ? Oh woods ! when, when shall I be made
> The happy tenant of your shade ?

Thomson's love of indolence and Cowper's partiality for a retired life are well-known. Nor have poets been less eloquent about the devotional aspirations stirred up by flowers. Listen to Wordsworth—

> Where will they stop those breathing powers
> The spirits of the new-born flowers ?
> They wander with the breeze, they wind
> Where'er the streams a passage find ;
> Up from their native ground they rise
> In mute aërial harmonies :
> From humble violet, modest thyme
> Exhaled, the essential odours climb,
> As if no space below the sky
> Their subtle flight could satisfy :
> Heaven will not tax our thoughts with pride
> If like ambition be *their* guide.

We have said that flowers are a beautiful analogy of the silent growth of the soul unto God. It was thus that our Saviour grew up secretly into the consciousness of his own divine nature. His hidden life is not meaningless. Slowly the bud expanded into the flower. From the first distinctive sign of that expansion conveyed in the words "Wist ye not that I must be about my Father's business" to the full bloom of God-life manifest in the flesh, this law of expansion or growth or development is distinctly traceable. Few there are who are able to say that time and meditation are of no special use to a life of faith. For short of miracle the process of sanctification in its practical bearings is a gradual process.

There is one other point in the words quoted as text

which requires explanation. Do not these words set a discount upon industry and toil? Do not they seem to foster sloth and immobility rather than persevering effort? We think this an entire misconception of their real meaning. There is no doubt that toil is of the curse pronounced on man : " In the sweat of thy face shalt thou eat bread." Yet St. Paul issues his admonition with much seeming severity, that if any work not, neither should he eat. Every wildflower points to the day when work shall be worship and labor shall be rest, when the believing spirit will be in uninterrupted and equable communion with the Spirit of God. All that is now enjoined, is an humble reliance in all our concerns on that Being who is at once the source and centre of all beauty and of all joy. " Seek ye first the kingdom of God and His righteousness, and all other things will be added unto you."

We love flowers when we are infants, when the " lilies look large as the trees ;" we are passionately fond of them in our schoolboy days, and we loiter in bye-lanes and beside hedges to pick them up ; and they exercise a genial influence on us when we grow old, instilling a summer feeling in the autumn and winter of our lives. Flowers are the poetry of the earth, as stars are the poetry of the sky. Flowers deck bridals, and are strewn over hearses. " We adorn their graves," says Evelyn, " with flowers and redolent plants, just emblems of the life of man, which has been compared in Holy Scriptures to those fading beauties whose roots being buried in dishonour rise again in glory."

To us who have been called out from the darkness and barbarities of heathenism, what a comforting assurance is it that our graves will be green with grass and blossom with flowers! Surely if there was nothing more in Christianity than this respect for the dead and this appreciation of the tender and the beautiful, it would justify our acceptance of that faith. But thanks be to God that there are things incomparably higher, incomparably more precious than these ephemeral mementos. For while the Christian's grave is decked with ever-greens and flowers, he himself will be crowned with wreaths of the immortal amaranth in the regions of light and blessedness, he himself will be transplanted to those bright parterres where grows in perfect beauty the Rose of Sharon!

Theocracy.

The Lord shall reign for ever and ever.—Exodus 15. (18).

God is the King of kings. All nations which profess Christianity acknowledge this. And though the Statute Book of such nations may contain laws which are against the intent and scope of the Bible, or the doctrines held may be some corrupted form of true religion, or the conduct of individual members and masses may deviate widely from it, yet the fact remains that wherever Christianity is the national religion,

God is acknowledged, nominally at least, as King. It has been often urged, and we believe with good reason, that this acknowledgment merely increases a nation's responsibility, and that thus, its lapses, faults and sins will be visited with punishment more condign. But at present we shall not enter into the invidious enquiry. That which is noble, that which is beautiful, that which is heavenly, must be acknowledged to be such. It matters not that every heathen monarch is not wicked like Domitian, who assumed the title of deity, and at the same time amused himself by sticking flies on a bodkin, or that every Christian monarch has not the wisdom and the lowliness of King Canute, renowned alike in story and in song—

"Then Canute, rising from the invaded throne,
Said to his servile courtiers,—" poor the reach,
The undisguised extent of mortal sway !
He only is a king and he alone
Deserves the name (this truth the billows preach,)
Whose everlasting laws sea, earth and heaven obey..

This just reproof the prosperous Dane
Drew from the influx of the main,
For some whose rugged mouths would strain
At oriental flattery ;

And Canute (fact more worthy to be known)
From that time forth did for his brows disown,
The ostentatious symbol of a crown ;
Esteeming earthly royalty
Contemptible as vain."

Yet the acknowledgment by a nation of God as King is after all, a noble, a beautiful, a heavenly thing. " Sir," said Archbishop Sancroft to the licentious Charles Second on his death-bed, "it is time to speak out ; for you are about to appear before a Judge who is no respector of persons." The world may be able to boast of an exceedingly limited number of Sancrofts, yet we would rather see it nominally Christian, than under the black sway of heathenism or other forms of false religion.

Theocracy means the royal rule of God over His people. The Old Testament theocracy commenced when God had revealed himself on Mount Sinai and Scripture became a written word, reached its point of culmination during the times of David and Solomon, and was entirely suspended by the destruction of Jerusalem. The New Testament theocracy has yet to be seen in its full development in the last epoch of the world-times, when Israel shall be converted and take the lead among the nations. As the institutions of the levitical service were promulgated to serve as types of Christ, so the Old Testament theocracy may be viewed as a type of the New, which will be the greatest glory on earth. The culminating point of the Old Testament theocracy, that is to say the times of David and Solomon, is thus in a peculiar sense a type of the kingdom of the Messiah, hereafter to be established. We have often heard objections taken against Scripture because David, who was guilty of flagrant crimes, is regarded by Christians to be a type of the Saviour, but except in the general sense above indicated of the puissance of his regal sway, and except in so far as he was led by God to do what is noble and just and proper, he is no more a type of the Saviour than a chimpanzee is a type of man.

The reigns of David and of Solomon are undoubtedly the most glorious era of Jewish history. "Saul," says the learned Heeren, "had only been the general of an army carrying out the orders of Jehovah as transmitted by Samuel, without a court, without a fixed residence. The nation was as yet only an agricultural and pastoral race, without riches, without luxury, but which became by insensible degrees a warlike people. Under David were effected a total reform of the nation and change of the mode of government ; the establishment of a fixed residence at Jerusalem, where was also the seat of the sanctuary ; a rigorous observance of the worship of Jehovah as the exclusively national religion ; a considerable increase to the State by conquest." But these conquests, however glorious, were excelled by the victories of peace, for " peace hath her victories no less than war," which were achieved in the reign of his son Solomon. Then " Judah and Israel dwelt safely, every man under his own vine and under his own fig tree from Dan to Beersheba." Then rose the great temple with the rapidity of the prophet's gourd. Every sort of oriental gorgeousness was lavished upon it,— works of bronze, iron, gold, silver and marble. And in the eighth year after the commencement, the Ark of the covenant was placed in the Holy of Holies. Some of the words of Solomon at the dedication are too remarkable to be omitted. " Will God," he said, " in very deed dwell with men on the earth ? Behold the heaven and the heaven of heavens cannot contain Thee ; how much less this house which I have built." !

And now we may remark in passing with reference to these words of King Solomon that the doctrine of the presence or omnipresence of God is often misunderstood in our days. The *locality* and the *essentiality* of the matter is mixed up, and thus a confusion begins. God is locally present only in the highest heaven, (and we do not know what or where that is,) but is essentially present in all that we see of nature's laws, and also in our own souls. Any deviation from this sound way of thought would land us on the shoals and quicksands of Pantheism. Poets may be allowed to say of changing seasons,

> "These as they change, Almighty Father, these
> Are but the varied God."

But when subjected to the test of true philosophy, the words will be found to mix up nature with nature's Author. In the beauty, symmetry and sublimity of nature, in the majestic mountain, in the broad river, in the life-giving breeze, in the simple wayside flower we trace God's pre sence, inasmuch as they are God's handiwork, and He sustains all that He has created. But to say that God is present locally anywhere but in heaven, is unsound. Even the Jewish people could only boast of the Shechinah.

But while acknowledging the presence of God everywhere in the sense above explained, we cannot at the same time be less sensible of the disturbing influences which exist both in nature and in ourselves. Hurricane, drought, famine and death, affect alike nature and man. By what spiritual influences these occur, we need not stop here to enquire. The glorious liberty of the children of God by which the creature itself shall be delivered from the bondage of corruption, shall be an accomplished fact at the ushering in of the New Testament theocracy.

And this leads us to speak about the glorious doctrine of theocratical liberty. Every Christian is a freedman of Christ. God is his king, and he is a priest and king unto God. And although we wait for the redemption of our bodies or transfiguration of the flesh, we are yet freedmen. Saved by hope, we care not for the disturbing agencies in creation, we care not for the evils which surround us, we defy Satan and his legions. We desire only the liberty in

Christ. As well might the lark, tumbling joyously over sun-lit morning clouds and pouring a full tide of song, envy the liberty of the strutting fowl; as well might the eagle, soaring high on the blue ether of the empyrean heavens, envy the liberty of the carrion kite or jay, as a Christian sigh for political freedom. Conscious of being the possessor of a far higher liberty it seems so comparatively valueless in his eyes, such a childish· trinket or gew-gaw, and composed of such weak and beggarly elements, that he has no thoughts to bestow upon it. This doctrine of theocratic liberty is at once the most consoling, elevating and salutary. Accept it, dear friends, and let a portion at least of your time and energies, spent in senseless political agitation, be consecrated to the cause of Christ.

Theocracy then has yet to be established in its glory and its fulness in this world. The day when this shall be, is known only to the Lord. But from the aspect of nature and from the events now occurring around us, it does not seem to be far distant. As there were large accessions in the shape of territory to the kingdom of David, so there will be large accessions to the kingdom of God. As there was a glorious temple in the time of Solomon, so there will be a temple far more glorious when the Lord shall reign in righteousness. God will dwell among men. Whether by Shechinah, or by out-pouring of the Spirit, or by local presence, we shall not presume to decide. The words are "He will dwell with them and they shall be His people." The temple will be a living temple. The materials are now being severed from the quarry. "My word," saith the Lord, "is as the hammer, and as the fire which breaketh in pieces the rocks." And again, "I will lay thy stones with fair colors, and lay thy foundations with sapphires, and I will make thy windows of agates, and thy gates of carbuncles, and all thy borders of pleasant stones." And from out this living temple will proceed the song " Alleluia, Alleluia, for the Lord God omnipotent reigneth" !

The Character of Christ.

My beloved is white and ruddy, the chiefest among ten thousand...................his countenance is as Lebanon, excellent as the cedars. His mouth is most sweet: Yea, he is altogether lovely.—SOLOMON'S SONG 5. (10—15,16.)

LET us contemplate for a little while the character of Christ. Nothing else can come up to it in beauty or sublimity. Shallow we must pronounce that philosophy to be which says, that beauty is no external entity, but is an affection of the mind, and of the mind only. It lies entangled in the web of its own wordy lore, and no eternal truths like what we see in the calm depths of Bible-philosophy, is to be found in it. As well might one say that heaven is a state and not a place, that the soul exists without the body raised out of corruption into incorruption, that spiritual life is a word without meaning, and not life as we know it, intensified, purified, sublimed, by grace from

on high, as that beauty is no external entity. It is true
that all objects present to our senses derive their beauty
from association, but what is the standard to which the
associated feelings conferring the adornment, refer? God is
beauty and Christ is God.

> ————"Fair the vernal mead,
> Fair the high grove, the sea, the sun, the stars,
> True impress each of their creating Sire !
> Yet nor high grove, nor many-colored mead,
> Nor the green ocean with his thousand isles,
> Nor the starred azure, nor the Sovran Sun,
> E'er with such majesty of portraiture
> Imaged the supreme beauty uncreate
> As thou meek Saviour" !

Childhood, manhood, death, the very perfection of beauty,
the very transcendence of sublimity.

Who can depict the beauty of the Babe of Bethlehem !
Raffaele made the attempt over and over, but could not suc-
ceed or even satisfy himself : the wise men of the east, bringing presents of gold and frankincense and myrrh, saw that
surpassing loveliness and worshipped : old Simeon felt its
benign influence when he took the Christ-child up in his
arms and uttered those memorable words. Nor was it a whit
tarnished when at the age of twelve he sat in the temple in
the midst of the doctors, both hearing them and asking
questions, engaged about his Father's business, but returned
with Joseph and Mary and was subject unto them. It shone
forth years after when the panegyric pronounced by a woman " Blessed is the womb that bare thee and the paps which
thou hast sucked," elicited the reply " Yea, rather blessed
are they that hear the word of God and keep it."

Christ has been styled " the first true gentleman that ever
breathed" by one of our ancient English poets. And separat-

F

ing the miraculous or divine element of his character, no truer
description of that character can anywhere be found. Now
the meaning of the word "gentleman" it is somewhat diffi-
cult to determine. It is different with different peoples, and
vary with varying circumstances. In Bengal or Bengali
Society Proper, no one is considered a gentleman who does
not possess a stagnant complaisance of temper, who does not
pucker his big well-shaven cheeks and relax his handsome
moustache-mounted physiognomy into a reverential grin at
all times, and at everything, who has not a great respect for
the conventionalities of life, for the Brahmins, and the gods.
Among the rising or advancing generation of Bengalis
called Young Bengal, a thorough contempt of caste and
all religions, and a turn for politics are perhaps the *sine
qua non*. In England and some other civilized countries
first-rate education is now an indispensable. And there was
a time when the term "gentleman" was synonymous with a
duellist, a horse-jockey, or a libertine. In no such tortuous
sense was our Saviour a gentleman, His was the highest,
holiest gentlemanhood. Condescension, wisdom, purity, love,
made up his life. Oh, how weak, how utterly jejune does all
other philanthropy appear compared with the philanthropy of
Christ. Who has or ever can more truly sympathise with
the world's sufferings ? All attempts to alleviate the miseries
of slavery, to raise humanity from vice and degradation, to
feed the hungry, to house the homeless, and clothe the naked,
are faint approximations to the *mind* of Christ. But there
are people who hold a different opinion. The injunction
"heal the sick, cleanse the lepers, raise the dead, cast out
devils, freely ye have received freely give, provide neither
gold nor silver, nor brass in your purses, nor scrip for your

journey, neither two coats, neither shoes nor yet staves"
issued at first under a restriction based on judicial reasons,
but which restriction was soon after expressly taken off, is
not enough to satisfy them. Glancing the other evening at
a work which on publication had a run of several editions,
'Ecce Homo,' we came across the following passage : "We
are advanced by eighteen hundred years beyond the apostolic
generation. All the narrowing influences, which have been
enumerated, have ceased to operate. Our minds are set free,
so that we may boldly criticise the usages around us, knowing them to be but imperfect essays towards order and happiness, and no divinely or supernaturally ordained constitution
which it would be impious to change. We have witnessed
improvements in physical well-being, which incline us to
expect further progress and make us keen-sighted to detect
the evils and miseries that remain. The channels of communi-
cation between nations and their governments are free, so that
the thought of the private philanthropist may mould a whole
community. And finally we have at our disposal a vast
treasure of science, from which we may discover what physical
well-being is, and on what conditions it depends. In these
circumstances the Gospel precepts of philanthropy become
utterly insufficient." Gospel precepts of philanthropy utterly
insufficient ! Is not the above passage Babylonish jargon ?
It requires no comment. It only reminds us of the Bengali
Baboo who came to us and said that he was prepared to
accept Christianity if we could prove to him that Christ's
commands for turning the right cheek when smitten on the
left, and of giving one's cloak when the coat is taken, are not
subversive of the best interests of society.

We will repeat then that Christ's character, regarded even

in its human aspect, is unequalled in excellency. The character of the Greek philosopher Socrates has sometimes been compared to the character of Christ, but the comparison only heightens the contrast. What, indeed, are his teachings in the groves of Academus, or on the banks of the Ilissus, beside the Sermon on the Mount? " Blessed are the poor in spirit: for theirs is the kingdom of heaven. Blessed are they that mourn : for they shall be comforted. Blessed are the meek : for they shall inherit the earth. Blessed are they which do hunger and thirst after righteousness : for they shall be filled. Blessed are the merciful : for they shall obtain mercy. Blessed are the pure in heart : for they shall see God." Did words like these ever fall from his lips ? To say the least it is foolish to make the comparison. Nor is the contrast at all less glaring when the closing scenes of the two lives are brought together. While Plato covered his face, Crito wept, and Apollodorus broke forth into lamentations, the words of the celebrated philosopher were ' What do ye my friends ? Truly, I sent away the women for no other reason, but lest they should in this kind offend. For I have heard that we ought to die with good men's gratulation, but recompense yourselves and resume your courage and resolution." This consolation to his disciples may be said to bear a distant, and almost imperceptible analogy to the words of Christ, " Daughters of Jerusalem weep not for me." But as we read further on, what vastidity of difference ! The last words of Socrates were " We owe a cock to Æsculapius ; but do ye pay him and neglect not to do it." The last words of Christ were ' Father, into thy hands I commend my spirit.'

We shall conclude by asking who *is* Christ whose character surpasses in beauty all other characters in history, nay all other characters in romance, ancient or modern? So that one more excellent has not even entered into the imagination of man : and by replying—Christ is God.

Atonement.

" Christ our passover is sacrificed for us."—1 COR. 5. (7.)

THE doctrine of the Atonement is the central truth of Christianity. Volumes have been written upon it with such ability, erudition and unction, that it is with the greatest diffidence that we undertake to say a word on this glorious and momentous theme. If the whole of the Bible were a myth, then indeed might the Socinian mode of explaining away this truth of truths appear plausible, but if the Bible be a record of verities, if it be a scroll in which we can trace types and symbols of higher truth, if it be a mine of inexhaustible spiritual treasure, then must the doctrine be accepted as set forth, without any attempt to accommodate and adjust it to our own weak and deluded ideas.

But before entering into an explanation of the Scriptural view of this subject, we may be allowed to observe that the religion of the Hindus gives a most prominent place to penances for sin, and though clearly open to a charge of frivolity on this account, it may thus be said to contain the doctrine of atonement in an embryous or corrupted state. According to the fanciful Angira " As the sun disperseth and removeth darkness, so penance disperseth and removeth sin. Even as the moon emerges from black clouds, so does a man emerge from his guilt by the performance of penance." To preserve the soul from the effects of *atipataka*, *mahapataka*, *upapataka*, *&c.*, presents to Brahmins, ablutions in sacred streams, and the repetition of mantras are enjoined." " A holy river," says the Mahabharata, "possesses the power of cleansing iniquities, numberless though they be, as surely as fire possesses the power of igniting cotton." Guatama and Viswamitra advocate presents of gold, clothes, cows, lands, horses and rice. A Brahmin killing another by accident has to make expiatory presents of 180 cows, but a Sudra guilty of the same offence, has to give away 720. Details of this description are given with a minuteness quite edifying.

Now, for the Scripture view. The book of Leviticus, which is the Statute Book of Jewish ceremonial law, contains, *inter alia*, the following directions for burnt offerings. " If any man of you bring an offering unto the Lord, ye shall bring your offering of the cattle, even of the herd and of the flock. If his offering be a burnt sacrifice of the herd, let him offer a male without a blemish......And he shall put his hand upon the head of the burnt offering, and it shall be accepted for him to make atonement for him." Now, comparing this clause with the language of St. Peter when he says " Redeemed with the precious blood of Christ, as of a lamb without blemish and without spot," it is to us a matter of profound wonder, that men should regard the analogy between the type and antitype, as forced or unsatisfactory, or inconsistent with the character of God. Of the essential attributes even of material things we know little or nothing, how then—of God? We can only know him as He has been revealed unto us. And the voice of this revelation is clear and decided on the point at issue.

The deeper and clearer our insight into the character of God, the deeper and clearer will be our view of the Atonement. God is love. God is purity. With infinite compassion for the sinner, he has infinite hatred against sin. In order, therefore, to open up a way for the sinner to be reconciled, he "became sin," that is to say, purity bore willingly the punishment of sin to rescue the sinner. The punishment, the pain, the agony, is the atonement made for man.

The objective manifestation of this truth is Christ on the Cross. The death of our Saviour was no ordinary death. The inspired Evangelist says that "at the ninth hour he cried with a loud voice, saying Eloi, Eloi, lama sabacthani?" His travail was in direct ratio to the holiness of his nature. Even for human beings death is horribly abnormal, it is sin working in us and culminating in a cessation of the vital functions, and unless superseded by the gift of new life is certain damnation. What must it then have been to the immortal Son of God! For a being of infinite purity and holiness, to suffer this condemnation, (or to use more mystical language) for God Himself to be separated from God, involved suffering which no human mind can fathom. He was "the Lamb slain from the foundation of the world." Out of infinite love God gave his Son to be a propitiatory sacrifice for the sins of the world. Through this propitiatory sacrifice the death in us may be supplanted by life. Almighty love has willed it so, even from the foundation of the world. Looking to that Cross and that bleeding Sacrifice, the Christian may well say, "death is swallowed up in victory."

Such then are the broad outlines of the doctrine of Atonement, a doctrine clearly read in Scripture, and without which Christianity would be an empty husk void of life or substance. It bears upon it the unmistakeable stamp of a divine original. It was God who planned it. His eternal attributes, He could not militate. Therefore, rather than lose the guiltiest of his creatures, the sword of vengeance awoke against His Fellow, and thus His justice was vindicated, and its glory magnified. High as this plan is, it reaches the darkest depths of human nature. No other plan except this "which the angels desire to look into" could have softened ossified souls or made 'dry bones live.'

"Christ our Passover has been sacrificed for us." The feast of the Passover or of unleavened bread was, as we all know, one of the three great festivals of the Jews. "Three times thou shalt keep a feast unto me in the year. Thou shalt keep the feast of unleavened bread : (thou shalt eat unleavened bread seven days as I commanded thee in the time appointed of the month of Abib ; for in it thou camest out from Egypt, and none shall appear before me empty :) and the feast of harvest, the first fruits of thy labors, which thou hast sown in thy field : and feast of ingathering, which is in the end of the year, when thou hast gathered in thy labors out of the field. Three times in the year shall all thy males appear before the Lord God." Exod. 23 (14-17.) These feasts were formal recognitions by the nation of God as King and Ruler and as the giver of every good gift, and had a most salutary influence on the national character ; they were also accompanied by such imposing solemnities as to render them types or exponents of their own peculiar religion. The Passover was celebrated by a sacred supper. A lamb was roasted and eaten with a salad of bitter herbs. Loins girt, staff in hand and kneading trough on shoulder, the guests partook of it. The bread was unleavened, and the utmost strictness was observed to remove all leaven from the house.

And now we shall conclude by observing the difference between *man's* religion and *God's* religion, between Hinduism and Christianity. " Christ our Passover has been sacrificed for us." Not what we have to do to expiate our sins, as in the religion of the Hindus, but what has been done for us is here expressed. Not a jot or tittle more is required. It is not Christ *helping* us even, but Christ *for* us. John Gerhard, a Lutheran divine, has well observed in a book published in 1606, "the Devil terrifies me with my sins, but let him accuse Him which hath undertaken my infirmities, whom the Lord hath smitten for my sins." Look then unto the Cross and be ye saved,—there is our Atonement, there our Surety.

The Jurisdiction of Science.

(An address delivered to the students of the Cathedral Mission College, 4th May 1872. By H. C. Dutt.)

SCIENCE and Scripture are often thought to be at variance. A belief in the conclusions of Science is supposed to be incompatible with a belief in the truths of Christianity. But do we rightly estimate the jurisdiction of Science? Scientific truths are not the only truths which have authority in this universe. Science cannot modulate the workings of the human heart. Mechanics tells us nothing about the soul, or Algebra about God. The spirit of man sees further than the telescope of the astronomer. No doubt Science is a glorious tool in the hands of man, but it has also its theories and its hypotheses which are made much too much of. One scientific man invents a theory to account for certain phenomena in nature, and another rejects it and supplants it with his own. Yet each in its time or turn bears the general *nom de guerre*, Science. The unseen world which we feel with our hearts and imaginations, the God whom we call Father, the holy Scriptures which we believe as true, are not subject to the domain and jurisdiction of Science. We know that scientific men who are infidels will accuse us of *begging the question*. But we might just as well retort this charge upon themselves. To believe that any thing exists outside our thoughts is in itself an act of faith. What is there to prove that all the things that we see around us are not visible and tangible portraitures of our own thoughts, or that we exist at all and do not merely think that we exist ? Nothing. All our reasonings would be essentially erroneous and defective if we left out of them altogether the important element of faith. Yet faith is not credulity, nor superstition, nor foolishness. Nay, it is the very opposite of all these. Because I believe that by taking ship I can in about forty days reach an island where during certain months of the year the water of tanks and rivers becomes so solidified that one may walk over it with ease, it by no means follows that I believe all that happened to Sinbad the sailor in his seven celebrated voyages. Because I am a worshipper of the Lord Christ it by no means follows that I worship the *avatars* described in the Hindu Pantheon. Because I admit the possibility, nay probability, of spiritual agencies and influences it by no means follows that I credit all the absurd ghost-stories invented to frighten or cozen children. Because I believe in a God it by no means follows that I accept all sorts of ideas about Him—Vedantic, Buddhistic, Brahmic. Faith is discriminative. Faith is wise. Faith is firm. Faith is everlasting. "Faith is the substance of things hoped for, the evidence of things not seen."

That Science has a jurisdiction subordinate to true religion will be patent even from this simple fact. Natural philosophy traces all external phenomena to Force or Law, whereas religion ascribes them to Force or Law guided by a Supreme Will. Thus the true religionist stands on a higher platform than the mere scientific man, and his view is therefore more far-reaching. Again, the physiologist declares that all feeling is inseparably bound up with the convolutions of the brain and with nerve-centres. But though a definite thought has its corresponding molecular action in the brain, no other relation can be traced by him between the two things than their simultaneity. He cannot therefore have any thing to say against a soul or impalpable spiritual body. True religion does not deny that thought and form in man are closely connected with one another. On the contrary it seems to support the theory. It speaks of the resurrection of the body, of a spiritual body to be eliminated out of the decayed or decaying elements of the gross body, and thus, like a higher court, adds to and confirms the deduction of Science.

The central truth of Christianity is beyond the jurisdiction of Science. "God manifest in the flesh" is a truth which Science dare not presume to analyse or explain scientifically. We may prove the possibility, the necessity, and the glory which await upon this truth. But we cannot by any means subject it to the test of the alembic. The chemist will shew that oxygen and hydrogen in fitting proportions with the combining touch of electricity form water, but what know we of God and of man to be able to shew how "the Word was made flesh and dwelt among us." It would be the very height of foolishness to attempt to do so. No. It is a truth which soars far above the domain of human science. It is a truth which flows down from heaven to earth in eddies of light. It is a truth which has heights inaccessible and depths unfathomable by the mightiest intellects yet pervaded by a divine simplicity which a "wayfaring man, though a fool," need not be at a loss to apprehend. It is a truth which shall encompass the whole earth in wave-like undulations, casting down all the strong-holds of superstition and triumphing over all the shoals and quick-sands of error. It is transcendentally glorious, expansive as the open horizon and serene as the pure blue sky.

Such also is that other truth, the truth of the Christian doctrine of atonement. It occupies an elevation whose height cannot be reached by the demonstration of the geometrician, or the telescope of the astronomer. Truly, faith has wings of mighty power. It mounts to the regions of the unseen and the eternal. Human laws know nothing about the punishment of the innocent for the guilty, in fact ignore and repudiate the very idea. But the glory of Christianity is that ."while we were yet sinners Christ died for us." The glory of Christianity is that human justice is not its emulative standrad. The glory of Christianity is that the righteous God, the Creator, veiling his God-head, undertook upon Himself the punishment that his fallen creatures deserved, that out of love He made atonement for the sins of mankind and thus magnified His own eternal law.

> " A humble form the God-head wore
> The pains of poverty He bore
> To gaudy pomp unknown,
> Though in a human walk He trod,
> Still was the man Almighty God
> In glory all His own.
> Despised, oppressed, the God-head bears
> The torments of this vale of tears,
> Nor bids His vengeance rise ;
> He saw the creatures he had made
> Revile His power, His peace invade,
> He saw with mercy's eyes."

Who among you then would be so foolish as to reject Christianity because its main truths cannot be proved scientifically ? Are they not beyond the jurisdiction of Science ? Is righteousness a fluid or a gas that we should be able to subject it to chemical processes ? Has man's moral nature veins and arteries that we should be able to dissect it anatomically ? Is eternity time that we should be able to measure it by the imperfect horologes by which we measure a day ? " The healthy understanding," says one of England's greatest thinkers, "is not the logical, argumentative, but the intuitive ; for the end of understanding is not to prove and find reasons, but to know and believe."

Regarding the discrepancies between some of the less salient truths of Christianity and the conclusions of Science, so called, which are ever and anon cropping up and occupying the attention both of the religious and scientific worlds, I cannot here speak at any length.* The author of the " Vestiges of the Natural History of Creation," Sir Charles Lyell, Darwin, and others are among the ranks opposed to the Bible. Though most of them do not profess to be open enemies of Christianity, they have collected data and drawn conclusions from those data, which if received as correct, destroy the credibility of the Mosaic account of the Creation. I have said I cannot enter upon a consideration of the differences now.

But I maintain that they are satisfactorily accounted for even by an admission of our imperfect understanding of the holy Scriptures and our imperfect knowledge of true Science. They are *seeming* discrepancies, and nothing more. The light of true Religion and the light of true Science proceed from one and the same God, and will eventually coalesce and shine unto the perfect day, and " God shall be all in all."

Have I depreciated Science ? By no means. I admit that Science even in its imperfect and progressive state is accumulating its benefits on man. It has prolonged life,

* The Saturday afternoon address at the C. M. College is usually restricted to fifteen minutes.

mitigated pain, annihilated distance, tamed the restless sea into a bearer of burdens, converted barren wastes into fruitful fields, circulated thought with the rapidity of thought itself, peered into the skies, dived into the depths of the earth, numbered the constellations, measured inaccessible heights, forestalled the winds, entrapped the subtle element of light even into its service, and made flowers to burst from their clod-beds with more enduring colors. New discoveries, new inventions are adding daily to our comforts and delectation, and bringing those comforts within easy reach of the poor. But over and above all this, Science rightly studied has an index-hand which points to the Great Creator. It is not for me to depreciate Science or to dissuade you from the study of the sciences. Science has its own jurisdiction. "Thus far shalt thou go and no further." Try to be sceintific men, eminent scientific men if you can, but never forget that Science is the hand-maid of Religion.

Christ set forth.

(An address delivered to the students of the Cathedral Mission College, 28th August 1875. By H. C. Dutt.)

JACOB BOEHME, the well-known German philosopher and mystic, accounts for the origin of evil in the following manner : He believes that this world was originally the glorious and celestial kingdom of Lucifer and his angels who were once holy and happy. Lucifer was the chief, but thinking it degradation to rule under sub-tenure to God, who is the Supreme, he tried to usurp authority and become independent. In this attempt he fell, and with him his angels, and his once glorious kingdom was shattered to chaos. The light and love of God being withdrawn, the fallen angels had nothing left in them but the fierce elements of fire, and wrath, and pride, and covetousness, and envy, and every hateful emotion of self-hood. On this ruined kingdom of Lucifer the mercy of God descended as we read in our Scriptures.

In the beginning God created the heaven and the earth.

And the earth was *without form and void : and darkness was upon the face of the deep.* And the Spirit of God moved upon the face of the waters.

And God said let there be light and there was light.

But the original possessors still endeavour to establish a right to the domain, and for this end exercise a very great but lamentable influence in stimulating human passions and swaying human beings who are placed in their fallen kingdom, to revolt from the authority of God.

I shall leave you to decide how far honest Jacob Boehme's views are correct. But you will, I hope, admit that we as human beings are in a state of alienation from God. We cannot of our ownselves act or think in a way pleasing to God. Each individual is after an illusion, chasing some fancied good, which, after all, may be no good at all. Some are for intellectual eminence, some for a great name, some for money-making, some for the pleasures of sense, some for sight-seeing, and so forth. The Yogis and Rishis of our country wanted to reverse somewhat the order of things, and to secure divine illumination by self-inflicted torments, but this was another illusion, and a very deadly one too. Seeing then that we cannot act in a way pleasing to God, that every one is gone out of the way, that all the thoughts and imaginations of our hearts are corrupt, that evil surrounds us and works within us, we naturally seek for help, and this help is vouchsafed to us in the Christian plan of Salvation.

Some eighteen hundred and more years ago there lived a man in Judea named Christ Jesus. The history of his life or ministry is fully set forth in four books which we call the Gospels. Looking into these and into certain other writings known as the Epistles and Revelation, we trace the origin of the existing Christian Church and the final destiny of nations. And not only this, but we trace therein such manifest proofs of God's holiness, of God's justice, of God's goodness, and of God's mercy, that we accept the writings as divinely inspired. The plan of Salvation and the way of life are clearly set forth in these writings.

Adam was created in a state of innocency and placed in the Garden of Eden as the representative of the whole human race. We were all in him when he fell. He fell, and " in Adam" we are told "all die." (1 Cor. 15. 22). Now some of you will say why should we, innocent fellows, suffer for the guilt or sin of Adam ; we were not even in existence at the time. Adam ate the fruit why should we feel its after effects ?—the pain, the misery, and the death. But let me tell you, or whoever these questioners or cavillers may be, that it is presumptuous thus to murmur against God. You might as well say why does God permit 'evil' to exist in the world. But we know that evil *does* exist, and God is not bound to give account of his matters to any. Well, Adam

H

fell. The world was ruined. For as his family, generation after generation, evolved out of him, each one possessed his father's fallen nature, for who can bring a clean thing out of an unclean? the world was ruined. But God loved the world, and would not leave it in a state of ruination. It pleased Him to stake it on another man who won back what the first man lost. St. Paul tells us that the first man is of the earth earthy, *only* a man though created without sin, yet a mere creature; the second Man is the Lord from Heaven. He was God and man. "God manifest in the flesh." (1 Tim. 3. 16.) Therefore He stood. And as all the family of Adam *died* in him, so all the family of God *live* in Christ. The believer belongs to both families. He lost his caste in Adam, he regains it in Christ. (So after all you see there is something about a *caste* question, though we know nothing of the *orders* sanctioned by Bullal.) He is born into Adam's family, heir to all his guilt, and misery, and corruption; he is received into the family of God through Christ Jesus (who is unto him wisdom and righteousness and sanctification and redemption), and thus becomes an heir to life, glory, and immortality, a very child of God. In Adam completely fallen, in Christ completely saved. In Adam completely sinful, in Christ completely righteous.

This then, my friends, is the Redemption wrought for us in Christ Jesus. Will you then, while accepting the progressive tendencies of the age in every direction, discard *the pearl* of great price! Would you not rather sell all you have and buy it, give up if need be all ideas of worldly advancement and worldly aggrandisement to become a disciple of the meek and lowly Jesus! The longest life is but a day, a grain of sand, a drop in the ocean, an insignificant unit in the equation of existence. But heaven is everlasting, and hell is everlasting, and eternity is everlasting, and God is everlasting, and the Redemption wrought for us is everlasting. Time flies and the chances of your being converted and becoming new creatures in Christ can only become less and less till on the brink of time and eternity you stand either a ruined or a made man, a child of wrath or a child of love! I speak as to wise men : Judge ye what I say.

Finally, my friends, the Scriptures tell us that not many wise men after the flesh, not many mighty, not many noble, are called, but God hath chosen the *foolish things* of the world to confound the wise, and God hath chosen the *weak things* of the world to confound the things which are mighty, and *base things* of the world and things which are *despised* hath God chosen, yea, and things which *are not* to bring to nothing things which *are*, so that no flesh may glory in his presence. In this God in Christ exercises his sovereign prerogative of mercy according to the good pleasure of his own will. *We* commonly select things on account of some natural aptitude for the purposes which they are to subserve, we never take an ugly, cross-grained, or worm-eaten piece of timber to make a pillar of state. But with God it is otherwise. He accepts as his own, and as his own by specialty, the poor, base, weak, foolish things of the world, the worst of men and chief of sinners. The instances of King David, of Paul, Mary Magdalene, and others, make this evident. And of such he is pleased to form vessels of honor, to be transfixt each in its right niche, standing columns in the house of God, whereon to inscribe in golden letters his *own* name, to manifest thereby his sovereignty, holiness, wisdom, power, righteousness, and free grace to Eternity !

George D'Amboise.

(*From the French of Monsr. Alex. Delavergne.*)

CHAPTER I.

1473.

It was one of the noble houses of Touraine, the house of the ancestors of Amboise, lords of Chaumont-sur-Loire. Pierre d'Amboise, the chief of that house in the fifteenth century, long a hardy captain, distinguished himself by high feats of arms during the reign of Charles VII. He was one of those who were chiefly instrumental in establishing that monarch on his throne and in chasing his foes from his realms, and had retired laden with honors and dignities to his Chateau de Chaumont for ending his days in peace, and superintending the education of a numerous progeny which his faithful wife Anne du Bueil had given him. He had seventeen children, eight sons and nine daughters, most of whom were living and in health in 1473. One day the old captain, used to the fatigues of war, feeling probably that his end was not distant, sent for his sons and addressed them in the following terms :

"My sons, you have up to this time conducted yourselves like gentlemen of high lineage, always occupied with horses, with arms, with falcons and with hunting, and I, young in mind though old in age, am most unwilling to withdraw you from these noble exercises ; but the time has almost come when it will be necessary for you to bid adieu to the house of your fathers, to the woods, to the fields, and to the beautiful river Loire, in order to go to Paris and present yourselves at the palace of the king your sire, and offer your services to him as become gentlemen. The time *is* come, my sons. But alas, I presumed too much upon the mercy of Divine Providence in thinking that I shall be permitted to throw myself at the feet of the king and present you myself. The wounds which my enemies inflicted have removed from me all my strength. It is but with a trembling hand that I could trace the letter supplicating the King Louis XI. to excuse an old servant of his father and offering him your services. The king did not make me wait for a reply. Look here!"

The Knight d'Amboise produced from his cincture a parchment sealed with the arms of France, and when, at a sign of his hand, his sons had approached according to the order of primogeniture, and had touched it with their lips, he opened it with solemn carefulness, and read with a grave voice, broken down by age and emotion, as follows:—

"Louis, the Eleventh by name, by the grace of God King of France, to his friend and faithful Chamberlain Pierre d'Amboise, lord of Chaumont, of Saint Cernin, and of other places, saluting.

Our very dear Chamberlain! We have received with pleasure your faithful letter, and lose no time in replying to it. We accept with open heart the offer which you have made us to consecrate to our royal service the eight sons with which heaven has blessed you, and, confiding in your proved loyalty and disinterestedness, we leave to your judgment the care of distributing among your children the offices, rank and honors, which the late King Charles VII., our father of blessed memory, had been pleased to bestow on you, reserving to ourselves the power of ratifying by our sanction all the dispositions which you might be pleased to make in the matter. Whereupon our faithful and beloved subject, let us pray to God that He keep you under His guardianship.

Executed in our royal hall of Tournelles on Thursday, the 10th April, of the year 1473.

Louis.

" Now then," added Amboise, " listen to what I have resolved, in order to conform myself as much as in me lies to the wishes of his majesty the king; unto you, Charles, who are the eldest, I give and bequeath my office of Royal Chamberlain; you Aimery, who are the second, I give and bequeath unto you the office of Grand Master of France, under this condition that you will proceed to the island of Rhodes and be among the Knights of the Order of St. John of Jerusalem in order to undergo there your novitiate; you Pierre, who are the third, I give and bequeath unto you my company of 200 armed men." Thus, when he had come to the turn of the eighth and last of his sons, a child of thirteen years, with a physiognomy full of intelligence and vivacity, the old lord of Chaumont emitted a deep sigh and cried—" As for you George, there remains for me nothing more to bestow; consequently my desire is that you enter the sacred order."

Here the Knight of Amboise made a pause for examining the impression which his words had made on his auditors. All eyes were fixed with interest on the young boy who, to the surprise of his brothers, did not betray the least sign of trouble or disappointment on his features; then, following their father's example, they knelt and devoutly recited their orisons. These concluded, the old captain, rising up with some effort, ensconced himself in his great arm-chair of sculptured oak, and thus terminated the conference with words which sounded like a solemn bell to the ears of his listeners :—"My sons, you have heard the wishes of the king by my mouth. Be you ready and depart early at break of day." All bowed respectfully and separated.

The next morning, at break of day, they presented themselves again in the chamber of their father, and, after having received his benediction and his injunction to shew themselves in all circumstances of life worthy of the high name they bore, mounted their horses in the court-yard of the castle. They were disposing themselves in order for passing the gate, when they met the son of the head butler of the castle, hat in hand and tears in his eyes. This young man had often joined in their sports, and had now come out to bid them farewell.

"John," said the eldest, as his horse gaily caracoled in his sight, "will you come with me to the court? I shall make you one of my esquires."

"No, master," replied the vassal, "I am the son of a servant, and am not fit for the court. God protect my good master."

"John," cried the second, "you speak with reason. Come after me and see the Grand Master of the Order of St. John of Jerusalem in the island of Rhodes. I shall see that you are received into one of the galleys of the order, belonging to the militia. You will be a soldier and afterwards captain."

"No, master," again replied the vassal. "How can I become a man of war, I, who am not able to see the death of a stag without shedding tears. God protect my good master."

Charles and Aimery and all the brothers having passed, with the exception of George, who was absorbed in something like a reverie during the foregoing dialogues, and seemed to pay no attention to them, the butler's son stood before him and said :—

" And you, my young master, how would you dispose of me ? Will you permit me to march in your company ?"

George gazed at his interlocutor with a puzzled countenance, and the two brothers, Charles and Aimery, retracing their grounds in order to be near the speaker, laughed heartily, and one of them added ironically—" And what would you, my poor John, that our brother the abbé will make of you ? perhaps a sacristan or a brother of the Mass ? " " That is all I want," replied the vassal with vivacity.

And taking up from the ground his baton and his knapsack, he prepared himself to follow the young abbé on the instant.

George blushed, shook himself on his stirrups, and having shot a fiery glance at his brothers, cried—

" Come, John, you have done well to follow me. My star is more brilliant than that of any of my brothers'. I bear under my cloak the destiny of the world."

He then added in a lower tone and in a mysterious manner —" I dreamt last night that I was the Pope."

Charles and Aimery laughed again, this time much louder than before, and recommenced their advance. George was not slow to join them. They were all on the same road for a time, but as it branched off, each took a last look of the towers of Chaumont, kissed the others, and went on his appointed way.

CHAPTER II.

1494.

ALL the steeple-bells of the city of Rouen pealed merrily, the streets were strewn with flowers, and the houses were hung with rich tapestries. A joyous crowd in holiday dresses reached up to the gates of the city and beyond the ramparts ; all the clergy of the metropolis, the sheriffs, and the association of tradespeople and merchants were waiting. For whom ? Mayhap for the King of France, or for the first prince of the blood, the Duke of Orleans, Governor of the province, or at least for the Legate of the Holy See. But no ? Charles VIII. was in Italy, and his cousin, the Duke of Orleans, had followed him thither ; the Holy See was in a state of flagrant hostility with the kingdom of France, and this honor cannot therefore be for the legate ;—all waited to receive simple George D'Amboise.

Many events had happened during the intervening twenty years. At first fortune was unfavorable to our young abbé who, while chaplain to Louis XI., had excited the suspicions of that dark monarch. Subsequently, when Charles VIII. had succeeded his father, George D'Amboise, associated with the ambitious projects of the Duke of Orleans, shared his captivity, and was on the point of losing his head by the hand of the common executioner. At last, after many vicissitudes, the wheel of the capricious goddess turned. He regained the favor of Charles, and was now about to exchange the petty bishopric of Narbonne for the diocese of Rouen and title of Primate of Normandy ; it was on this same day that he came to the possession of the riches and privileges which attached to this ecclesiastical dignity.

I

After having traversed the city amid the acclamations of the crowd and vapours of incense which they burned on both sides of his passage, the new Archbishop, flushed with triumph, stopped before the splendid palace which was to serve as his residence, and perceived, among a number of faithful people who had come to prostrate themselves at the gate for obtaining his blessing, a man of tall stature, dressed in a costume half ecclesiastical and half secular, hiding his face with his hands as if in deep emotion. He was the only one who was not kneeling, at which the others murmured, and some loud voices cried in a menacing tone—" On your knees, man! On your knees, pagan! On your knees, impious." On hearing these exclamations he, to whom they were addressed, hastened to comply, and, in doing so, one of his hands fell and partially discovered his countenance. George D'Amboise recognized with surprise John, the son of the butler of Chaumont castle, of whom he had lost sight during his captivity. Immediately advancing, he took hold kindly of his hand, introduced him with the suite into the interior of the palace, and recommended him to the care of the servants.

When all the brilliant cortege, which accompanied George D'Amboise on coming to his new possessions, had retired, the prelate, being alone, sent for his ancient companion of the road, and, after having embraced him with the utmost tenderness, said—

"Ah! my good John, you see you were not mistaken when twenty years ago you determined to follow me in preference to my brothers. You see me Archbishop of Rouen, and I do not mean to rest there. Know, that Cæsar Borgia, nephew of the Sovereign Pontiff, has promised me in his last letter a Cardinal's hat, so sometime, soon or late, my dream will be accomplished, and I shall be Pope.''

All the response which John gave was *tears*.

"What is it afflicts you, John"? asked the prelate. "Is it money? I am rich, and my purse is at your service. Are you afraid that you have offended by separating yourself from me when fortune was against me? I have forgotten all now that she smiles. I need an attendant as faithful as you have been, and I do not wish that you should quit me any more.''

"Excuse me, my lord,'' said the son of the butler of Chaumont, "I do not belong to myself, but am in the service of a community which has received my vows.''

"There is no community in France so powerful that George D'Amboise will not be able to dissolve the vows you might have made to it.''

"Alas! my lord, I do not desire it myself—give ear unto what I have to say. I came to Rouen not to witness your triumphal entry, nor to ask from you any grace or favor; it was only to see you once more before I die: I wished not even that I should be recognized by you, because I knew well that being recognized, I should feel great pain in leaving you. Excuse my boldness my lord, but when I betook myself to religion after your example, it was for my salvation. I had no other ambition than to serve you in the Mass (you whom I love so well) even to the end of your days. But you would not have it so, and loved better to become a prince of the Church. Heaven protect you in all your undertakings my lord, but I do not wish to be more than its humble servant here on earth. I am happy in my poor convent. Allow me to return thither, and I shall pray to God for you to the last hour of my life.''

On hearing these words George D'Amboise became thoughtful and pensive for some moments, and after a short silence rejoined with a voice trembling with emotion, " Brother, it is God who speaks by thy mouth, and I shall not allow you to part thus ; I wish you to see me to-morrow, and speak the same language which I have heard just now, and on which may depend the salvation of my soul ; I wish to sleep this night meditating on your words, then, brother, we may part in peace."

The next morning John presented himself, but the prelate was not visible, engaged probably in writing letters to Cæsar Borgia for the accomplishment of the promise of a Cardinal's hat. Others assisted John in distributing to the poor the purse of silver which he had received from his master, and in putting off the rich clothes which, as enjoined in the palace, he had to wear.

A few hours afterwards, on the road not far from Rouen, could be seen a figure in a costume half ecclesiastical and half secular, a stick in his hand and a wallet on his back, casting at times a furtive look at the city which he was leaving. It was brother John returning to his humble duties.

CHAPTER III.

1510.

ONE evening, in the month of May 1510, the gate of the convent of the Celestines at Lyons was knocked with violence, and as the brother in charge was slow in opening it, several voices from without cried—

" Help ! help ! open quickly to my lord the Cardinal, first minister, who is in danger of his life."

At these cries, and as the venerated name was pronounced, the gate turned quickly on its hinges, and a litter was introduced into the convent. He whom it contained was carried to a cell, the best that could be found, and after the medicines had been administered which his state urgently needed, a brother was searched out to take charge of the illustrious patient, who had fallen into a profound slumber, no doubt a salutary crisis in the malady. The brother thus entrusted with this important duty, had been roused hastily from bed, and found himself in that state, physically and mentally, which one may call neither waking nor sleep, and partook somewhat of the conditions of either. For it was not long after his introduction into the cell that he slipped mechanically from a doze to that profound slumber which had been so rudely interrupted, on the stool beside the patient's pillow. At about midnight the Cardinal awoke so as to be able to look about him, and by the dim light of the lamp which was burning, contemplated with interest the serenity and happiness which rested on the face of the sleeping attendant ; then rousing himself more fully as old remembrances thronged in his mind, he seemed to see in that face and in that capacious brow (now furrowed with a few wrinkles) the countenance of an ancient friend. He seized the attendant's hand and asked his name.

"My name is Brother John," said the man in accents hardly intelligible or audible.

"John of Chaumont-sur-Loire" ?

"The same —— you know me then" ?

" Ah," said the prelate with grief, " you have been a good deal changed, my good John, not to recognize George D'Amboise." The monk gave a cry, and fixing his eyes with surprise on the pale visage of the patient, fell on his knees.

" What is the matter, brother ?" asked the Cardinal.

" I pray heaven and you, my lord, to pardon me for having quitted so good a master."

" Ungrateful !" said the Cardinal smiling, after having raised himself a little. " Were you not happy at the Archbishopric !" I ordered that you should be treated there like my own self."

" Alas ! my lord, that was too good for me. What could I do among your luxurious clergy and your brilliant gentlemen. I rested at Rouen to see you, to speak to you, and I was interdicted from appearing in your presence. I liked better returning to the cloister, where I may see God whenever I please and speak to Him whenever I please.

" Then you are happy here"?

" Yes, my lord, because I am exempt from ambition and from care ; what I did yesterday I do to-day, and what I do to-day I will do to-morrow, till it please the Lord to take me hence."

" What have you to do" ?

" I pray to God and attend on my sick brothers."

" That is hard work."

" O no, because the sick are so few, and I feel so glad when they get well."

At this instant the voice of a trumpet resounded in the city.

" What is that"? said our lay brother, "what is it which causes such a loud fanfaron at this unseasonable hour ?" The Cardinal raised himself on his bed almost involuntarily, and a crimson flush appeared on his tired cheeks, where one could trace the symptoms of approaching dissolution. With some emphasis he articulated, " That, John ! that is the King of France! He and his nobles have reached Lyons, and will part to-morrow, if it please God, to chastise Pope Julius II. who has robbed me of the tiara.

" That's true," replied frankly the *religieuse*, " I remember now that you wished to be Pope."

George D'Amboise, fixing his eyes on the speaker and holding him by the hand, said with an air of undefinable sadness.—

" *Brother John, alas! that I have not been all my life Brother John !*"

A few days after this conversation, on the twenty-fifth May 1510, died in the same cell, and in the arms of the brother, the powerful Cardinal D'Amboise. His body was removed with great pomp into the Cathedral at Rouen, where it was buried in a magnificent tomb of marble, which is the admiration of all up to the present day ; but his heart rested in the Convent of the Celestines, where he had refound Brother John. Though during his life-time he had not shared the humble lot of that faithful *religieuse*, yet after death he shared his tomb.

POEMS.—RELIGIOUS.

Ahab.

(A Dramatic Fragment.)

Ahab.—King of Israel.	*Benhadad.*
Jezebel.—The queen.	*Naboth.*
Elijah.	*Jehoshaphat.*
Obadiah.	*Micaiah.*

Prophets, Soldiers, Messengers, &c.

Scene I.—The lawn before the ivory palace at Jezreel with its carved window overlooking the vast plain of Esdrae-lon, Carmel and other mountainous elevations at a distance. Time, evening. Jezebel alone......sumptuously appareled...

JEZEBEL.

——They call me proud
Nay, I am not proud—my father Ethbaal
Never crossed a wish of mine— he made me
What I am, and I—I am Ahab's queen,
Queen of proud Israel loth to bow the neck
To Baal.   But I shall see her tamed—I must.
These groves of olive and of ilex round
The rocks on which stand Israel's altars shall
Resound with praises of my father's gods
Baalim and Ashtaroth ! E'en now the first
In glorious vestments clad sinks out of sight,
Leaving a trail of brightness on yon clouds
And yonder western hills.   I love these clouds,

I love these silent hills, for they have charmed
Me oft with their transcendent loveliness !
Two rays, two mystic rays from yon hill-top
Seem darting towards me now, the one it says
Jezebel, thou art beautiful thyself,
The other says have courage, queen, and rule
With iron will.   These messengers are Baal's ;
I know it, feel it.   But soft, who comes here ?
A hairy man erect and tall, with beard
That flows down to his girdle, clad in skin.
His eyes are darting fire—the very sight
Makes me afraid—I will retire and send
The king to meet him.

(Retires into the palace.)

Ahab confronted with Elijah.

ELIJAH.

——As the Lord liveth,
No rain shall fall from heaven, but parching drought
Shall suck up all the moisture from the clods
Hardening to stone the plastic element ;
Nor grain nor grass shall grow, and the cattle
On your plains and hills shall bleat for pasture ;
Rivers and water-sheets shall be dried up
And turned to arid wastes, and hundreds die
Of thirst.   Beware O King !—Thus saith my God
Jehovah, Israel's God, and by my mouth.
Him hast thou insulted, Him not feared,
But at the instigation of thy queen
Reared a high altar in the house of Baal.
Beware, O son of Omri ! Thou hast dealt

Treacherously with the Lord and provoked
His wrath. I go. But what I say will come,
For He hath spoken. This sea of verdure
Which I see, now so full of sap and green,
Shall droop and die under a withering spell,
Nor shall the spring with breezes soft revive
Them into life, nor summer ripen them
To fruitfulness, nor autumnal tints paint
The sheaves for storing into granaries.
Beware ! Beware !——

*Scene II.—A dreary wild near the banks of the Jordan, with
heath and juniper bushes here and there. Further on,
naked rocks and forests terminating in a deep and nar-
row glen overhung with tangled wood. Brook Cherith
winds its devious course along the rocky masses.*

ELIJAH.

———Yes, here I am,
The blue sky my awning, the grass my couch,
This stone my seat, the waters of this brook
My drink, those ravens up among the trees
My kind feeders. God's Spirit led me here.
God is my shepherd, and I shall not want.
God feeds the ravens and the ravens me.
And to that brother prophet, who brought out
Israel from Egypt, and to whom were given
The tablets of the law, hath He not said—
" I suffered thee to hunger, and fed thee
With manna which thy fathers did not know,
Nor doth man live by bread alone, but by
Each word that cometh from My mouth ? "

What if one of the bushes which I see
Were to ignite like the one in Horeb,
Would I be surer of His voice than now?
O Jezebel! Jezebel! The prophets
Of the Lord hast thou without compunction
Cut off, till Obadiah hid the rest
By fifty in a cave, woe awaits thee!
Now in this noon-day heat, the broad shadow
Of this rock my shelter, I shall lift up
My voice and chant the words which Balaam spake
Of yore—" God is not man that he should lie,
Neither the son of man that he repents,
Hath he said and shall he not do the same?
The shout of a king is with him that fears
The Lord, and the strength of an unicorn
Is his."

Scene III.—A Chamber in the palace.   Ahab and Obadiah.

AHAB.

—Three years—three long years have past, the seasons
Have returned and gone, yet no drop of rain!
The thirsty glebes with mouths wide open lie
In unremitting fever and with nought
To satisfy their parched lips.   It is
The curse of that wild man, Obadiah,
That has brought this sore famine on the land
With its attendant train of pestilence.
And havoc of men and beasts.   Some more days,
And my fair kingdom will be but a pit,
A charnel-house for rotting carcases:
Go thou one way—I shall go another—

And should you chance to meet the man who thus
Doth trouble Israel, bring thou him to me,
And I shall see how his prophetic mood
May brook my royal presence.

OBADIAH.

King, I obey,
But take good heed that in thy foolishness
Thou dost not add sin unto sin.   The blood
Of the prophets thou hast slain already
Cries loud for vengeance—would you slay one more?

AHAB.

Nay, I shall not slay him,
But he and the prophets of Baal shall meet.
And those that eat at Jezebel's table
Shall also be there, and then all shall see
Who conquers, Baal or God.

OBADIAH.

King, I go.   As you bid I go,
But I shall always honor God's prophets.

*Scene IV.—The heights of Carmel.   Elijah and the prophets
of Baal, &c.*

ELIJAH.

How long halt ye betwixt two opinions ?
If God be God follow him, if Baal then
Follow him.————————————
I, e'en I only remain a prophet
Of the Lord, but ye, the prophets of Baal,
Are four hundred and fifty men.   Bring here
Two bullocks, choose ye one bullock

For yourselves, and cut in pieces, and put
No fire under ; I will dress the other,
And do likewise ; and call ye on the name
Of your gods, and I will call on the Lord,
And the God that answereth by fire, He is God.

PROPHETS OF BAAL.

Agreed ! Agreed !

AHAB AND HIS COURTIERS.

It is well spoken.

ELIJAH.

Choose ye one bullock for yourselves and dress
It first, for ye are many.

*Some of the prophets of Baal rush out and bring in a dressed
bullock and wood to place it on. The meat is placed on
the wood. Then the prophets divide themselves into par-
ties and cry continually—*

" O Baal hear us !" " O Baal hear us !"

ELIJAH.

Cry aloud, for he is a god. Either
He is talking, or pursuing, or on
Some journey, or peradventure he sleeps ;
Cry aloud for he is a god !

PROPHETS.

Baal ! Baal ! hear us.

ELIJAH.

It is the time of evening sacrifice,
Hath he not answered yet ?

PROPHETS.

(Discomfited.)

Nay, nay,
He has not answered.

ELIJAH.

Then come near unto me, O ye people ;
Here I rebuild the altar of the Lord
That was broken down—with these twelve stones
Rebuild I it—the twelve tribes of Israel
Thus I honor and acknowledge.   Now bring
The bullock and let me hew it on the wood ;
Fill four barrels with water and pour it
On the sacrifice and on the wood—do
It a second time, and once again—Fill
The trench with water—now stand back.

Lord ! whose throne is on the hills,
  Whose sceptre rules the sea,
In feeble accents thus I raise
  My suppliant prayer to thee,
Light sprung from gloom at thy command,
  And stars bedecked the azure plain,
The earth its garniture revealed
  Loud sang the billows of the main,
At thy command still through the year
  The woods in varied garbs appear.

When clouds in dense battalions lour,
  And darkening tempests rave,
We call Thee by thy name of power,
  For Thou alone canst save—

Speak but the word—flash after flash
    Shall light the drear abysmal deep ;
Speak but the word, and all at once
    The warring winds subside and sleep,
Heaven's concave with Thy praises rings,
    Lord of lords and King of kings !

Lord ! the God of Abraham,
    Here I pray this day
That fire fall on this sacrifice
    And bear the parts away.
Upon the everlasting sky
    No speck sails now, the earth,
Both Carmel heights and Sharon's plain,
    Are sick to death for moisture-dearth—
Let fire fall on the sacrifice,
    Thy glory pass before their eyes.

The fire of the Lord falls and consumes the sacrifice and the
    wood and the stones and the dust licking up the water that
    was in the trench. The people fall on their faces, saying,

    " The Lord is God !" " The Lord, He is God !"

ELIJAH *(to the people.)*

Take, take, bind
The prophets of Baal, let not one escape,
And I myself will bring them to the brook
Kishon and slay them there.   Hie thee, Ahab,
Back to thy palace, for I hear a sound
Of plenteous rain ; hie thee, from a speck
No bigger than a hand the rain will come
Till all the heavens are black with clouds and wind.

Scene V.—The Court of Ahab.—Ahab, Obadiah and other courtiers.

OBADIAH.

The Syrian host hath covered all our plains,
And from the heights their tents appeared to me
Like troops of white-winged sea-birds ; I approached
And the busy hum of men belonging
To the kings in league, the clank of armour,
And the loud neighing of their mettled steeds,
Left not a doubt in what guise they come.   King,
It is a terrible day for thee and all
Samaria !

(Enter Messenger.)

MESSENGER.

My lord, an ambassador
From the king of Syria asks admittance.

AHAB.

Admit him without let or parley.   I
Myself shall try to come to terms——

(Exit Messenger.)

Enter Ambassador.

AMBASSADOR.

Benhadad, King of Syria, thus through me
Speaks to the King of Israel.   I have come
With horses and with chariots and with men
You may not count to besiege thy kingdom ;

Thou shalt deliver up to me thy gold
And silver, thy wives and children, and all
That is most pleasant in thy eyes ; I send
My servants unto thee to-morrow, they
Shall search thine house and bring to me the best
Thou hast.   Syria, whose puissant sway extends
From Taurus to Arabia, from Cydnus
To the Euphrates, shall number Israel
As its tributary.

AHAB.

These are proud words, these are hard conditions—
Hard conditions !

OBADIAH AND THE COURTIERS.

King, agree not
To the least of them.   But repel with scorn
The base insulting speech ; hundreds of youths
Still live in fair Samaria whose blood
Courseth with martial ardour through their veins,
Who willingly would sacrifice their lives
For thee and for their country.

AHAB.

Nay, I doubt not ;—
Bear my defiance then to Syria's king ;
Tell him Samaria never shall be his,
Tell him Samaria's youths shall meet his host
(Mighty though it be) in battle.   Tell him
Our darts are keener edged than his, we wait
Upon the God of battles !

Scene VI.—The queen's bed-chamber. Ahab reclining on a royal bedstead, Jezebel sitting near him.—

AHAB.

The Syrians have been defeated and routed
At Aphek yet I am not happy ! O—
How happy would I be if I possessed
Naboth's vineyard, that I may plant therein
Sweet herbs ; it's so near my palace, so near !
I'd turn it to a garden and in the midst
Erect a summer-house o'er-lapped with leaves
And flowers, for thee and me, and at evening,
When birds are musical, we would sit there
And listen to their notes, and the lowing
Of the distant herds, and sip the grape-juice
From goblets rare, and take our fill of joy !
There would we see the golden butterflies
Chase each other, and know what 'tis to love.

JEZEBEL.

My own dear Ahab !

AHAB.

But Naboth is a covetous crusty rogue,
And does not yield ; he told me, " God forbid
That I should sell my father's heritage
To thee though thou be king." I felt his words
Like a bodkin pierce my soul, I gulped them
As a bitter draught, therefore am I sad.

JEZEBEL.

Ahab! Dost govern Israel,
And say for this thou'rt sad ? O foolish king,
Rise, eat bread, and let thy heart be merry.
I will give thee the vineyard of Naboth,
I will write letters in thy name, and seal
Them with thy seal, instructing the elders
And the nobles to bring false witnesses
Against the man that he has blasphemed God
And the king, and when the case is proved, they
Shall carry out and stone him that he die.

AHAB.

A woman's soul is stronger than a man's.

JEZEBEL.

Rise and eat, and let thy soul be merry.

Scene VII.—The vineyard of Naboth. Ahab and Elijah.

ELIJAH.

Thus saith the Lord,
Hast thou killed and also ta'en possession ?
There, where the doge licked the blood of Naboth,
Shall dogs lick thy blood, even thine.

AHAB, (*aside.*)

It is my old enemy Elijah,
He has found me out !

ELIJAH.

Because thou hast sold thyself
To work evil in the sight of the Lord,

The Lord hath said " I will cut off thy heirs
And make thy house like unto the house of
Jeroboam son of Nebat, or like
The house of Baasha son of Ahijah,
For the provocation wherewith thou hast
Provoked me to anger and made Israel
To sin." Of Jezebel also spake He, saying
" The dogs shall eat Jezebel by the wall
Of Jezreel." Beware ! Beware !

*Scene VIII.—A void place in the entrance of the gate of
Samaria, Ahab king of Israel and Jehoshaphat king
of Judah in their royal robes sitting on two thrones.
Prophets, courtiers, messengers, &c., ranged on either
side.*

AHAB.

I told thee, brother-king, Ramoth-Gilead
Is ours, yet the Syrians keep it from us,
And all the prophets gathered here this day
Have said, Go up to battle, for the Lord
Shall deliver it into our hands. But
There is yet one man, Micaiah, who should
Be consulted, he never prophesies
Good concerning me, him have I sent for,
And he must say in this assemblage, what
He doth think of our intended raid.

JEHOSHAPHAT.

I am as thou art, my men as thy men,
My horses as thy horses.

One of the prophets, Zedekiah, the son of Chenanah, with two horns of iron on his forehead, darts out from the crowd and presents himself before Ahab, saying—

"Thus saith the Lord
With these thou shalt push the Syrians until
    Thou hast consumed them."

The rest of the prophets cry out.

" Go up to Ramoth-Gilead
    And prosper,
" Go up to Ramoth-Gilead
    And prosper."

Enter Messenger and Micaiah.

MESSENGER TO MICAIAH (*aside.*)

Behold now the words of all the prophets
Have declared good unto the king, thy word
Should be like unto theirs, for thy own sake
Speak that which is good and no way evil.

MICAIAH.

As the Lord liveth,
What the Lord saith unto me that speak I.

AHAB.

What sayest thou ? Micaiah,
Shall we go up gainst Ramoth-Gilead
To battle, or forbear ?

MICAIAH.

Go and prosper, thou shalt win.

AHAB.

How many times must I adjure thee that
Thou tell me nothing in an irony,
But speak the truth as it doth come to thee.

MICAIAH.

(After a pause, fixing his eyes on vacancy.)

I saw all Israel scattered on the hills
As sheep without a shepherd ; the Lord said,
These have no master, let each return to
His own house in peace !

AHAB TO JEHOSHAPHAT *(aside.)*

Did I not tell thee
That he would not prophesy good of me ?

MICAIAH.

I saw the Lord sitting upon his throne,
And all the host of heaven standing on His
Right hand and on the left, and the Lord said
Who shall persuade Ahab that he go up
To Ramoth-Gilead and fall ? one said this
Another that, till a lying spirit
Came forth and stood before Him saying,
I'll persuade him ; the Lord then asked wherewith ?
And he answered, I will go forth and be
A lying spirit in the mouth of all
His prophets, now therefore, behold, the Lord
Hath put a lying spirit in the mouths
Of these thy prophets !

ZEDEKIAH, THE SON OF CHENANAH.

(Going near and smiting Micaiah on the cheek.)
Which way went the Spirit of the Lord from
Me to speak to thee ?

MICAIAH.

Behold, thou shalt see the day when thou shalt
Go into a chamber to hide thyself.

AHAB.

Take Micaiah and carry him back to
Ammon, governor of the city, say
Thus saith the king—Put this pestilent wretch
In prison, and feed him with bread and water
Of affliction, till I return in peace.—
Now to battle !

*Scene IX.—Ramoth-Gilead.   Trumpets at a distance.
Battle. Ahab in disguise on his chariot.*

AHAB.

The Syrian darts swim on the air in shoals,
Our troops retreat, the battle's well-nigh lost,
And I am wounded. Driver, turn thine hand
And carry me out of the host, the blood
Is gushing fast and I feel faint, carry
Me to the nearest pool and stanch this wound
And wash your chariot there. O the words of
That wild man are ringing in my ears,

I feel faint and fainter yet, I hope it is
Not death—O those words—Dost thou not hear them?
" *There, where the dogs licked the blood of Naboth,*
Shall dogs lick thy blood, even thine."
Drive hard? drive hard! Oh!

(Dies.)

Worship.

I walked the fields at break of day,
   And by the hedge espied
A small white flower, that bloomed alone
   In beauty—not in pride.

And down-dropt were the soft blue eyes
   Of that sequestered nun !
As fast advancing, streamed around
   The first light of the sun.

An air of pensiveness about
   Its modest worth was thrown,
And from its little heart arose
   A fragrance, all its own.

Ah ! few, said I, now know the spot
   Thou gracest silently,
And fewer yet shall mourn, fair flower,
   When thou wilt cease to be.

Methought the Spirit of the flower
   Did softly make reply,
'Though lonely, I am truly blest,
   I worship, and I die.'

Lines.

God, who in times of old communion held
With prophets and with sages, and inspired
Their spirits to foresee in waking dreams
The shadowed semblance of reality ;
Who from the Sacred Mount in thunders gave
The Law to Moses and the multitude ;
Who walked with Abraham, and at dead of night
Revealed His edict to young Samuel,
Speaks to us still if we but choose to listen.
The sky, the earth, the ocean's broad expanse,
The stars that burn, the seasons as they roll,
The blushing fruits, the flowers that deck the lawn,
The maiden rill that by the hamlet glides,
Have they not voices for the spirit's ear ?
The wind that stirs, or the mad hurricane
That lasheth waves to fury and subsides,
The mountain-echo and the lonely tarn,
The twilight's glow that fills the earth and heaven,
Have they not voices for the spirit's ear ?
Nor these alone, but Nature animate
Attest the *presence* of a living God.
How cunningly the swallow 'neath the eaves
Builds her small nest.   Who guides the busy bee
From flower to flower ?—who gives to butterflies
Their wings of light to skim the liquid air ?
The song of birds, when morning paints the skies,
The stock-dove's coo at noontide's death-like calm,

The plash of fishes in the clear moonlight,
The cricket's chirp beside the blazing hearth,
The oft-seen faces of the friends we love,
The prattle of fair children in their play
(Those household angels sent from God above),
Have they not voices for the spirit's ear?

God speaketh now as in the days of yore
He spake to holy men, while Nature's book
His power, His wisdom, and His love reveals :
And had not sin deadened the sense of our
Ethereal substance, rendering it akin
To grosser clay, more should we surely hear.
In each event of life God speaks—from Him
Afflictions come and not by accident.
When stretched on bed of sickness or of pain,
'Tis He supports the sinking spirit—breathes
Words of comfort, and bids us to review
Our every thought and deed, and thus prepare
To meet Him ' face to face'—'tis He commands
Each noble impulse of the soul and cries
' Well done' to workers of His will.   Of old
Our fathers had no higher privilege
Than we have now—God spake to them, God speaks
To us, and all things shall be well if we
Obey His voice, and patiently submit
To His decrees in faith, and hope and love.

John X. 14.

Green are Thy quiet pastures, Lord,
   The waters clear and still,
Oh, thither lead Thy thirsty flock
   By Zion's holy hill !

For there Thy Sun of Righteousness
   Makes ever perfect day,
And clouds of sin and error fade
   Before His searching ray.

No habitations made with hands
   Uprear their columns high,
But all may rest beside the Rock
   Or 'neath the glorious sky.

Eye hath not seen nor heart conceived
   The beauty of the scene ;
Unfading are the flowers that bloom
   Amid those pastures green.

Drink of those streams and never more,
   My soul ! thou'lt thirst again ;
Breathe but for once that ambient air
   And banish fear and pain.

To those calm regions of the blest,
   Good Shepherd, be my guide ;
And all my weary journey through
   Walk ever at my side.

I John IV. 16.

The glowing sun and planets pale
  That through the trackless ether move,
Where'er they shine, with silent voice
  Tell wondering millions—God is Love.

The varying seasons sing of God,
  Dark clouds proclaim Him from above ;
The wintry frost, the summer heat
  Alike declare that God is Love.

The air we breathe—our onward lives,
  Our varied blessings surely prove,
There is a heart that yearns for man,
  There is a God whose name is Love.

The open lawn—the flowering woods,
  Where oft at eve I love to rove,
In softest language, seem to say
  To my sad spirit—God is Love.

The waving palms that shade the stream,
  The sweet-voiced warblers of the grove,
Raise choral songs in unison
  With Nature's echo—God is Love.

And thou blest Cross of Calvary,
  Stained with His blood whose Life was Love,
The glorious tidings bring'st to all,
  ' Believe and live, for God is Love.'

Fear not.

'Fear thou not.'—Isaiah xli. 10.

Fear not, mortal! though thy path
  With gathering clouds be dim ;
Not unwisely, but to chasten,
  Sorrows come from Him.

Bewildered? Helpless? pray for aid,
  And aid will sure be given ;
From among those clouds shall break
  Light from heaven.

Though the world be all against thee,
  Though hast still a Friend ;
The vastness of whose tender love
  None can comprehend.

Blessed spirits will attend
  And smooth thy bed of pain,
Yes, peace and healing flow from them
  Calming heart and brain.

Fear not Death—the dark transition
  To a happier sphere,
Where the flowers bloom more lovely,
  And the skies are clear.

For Sin is gone—Christ died to save
  The sheep that went astray ;
And souls that turn to Him in truth
  He never casts away.

Look upon thy Saviour, mortal,
  Mark the thorn-crown round His brow,
And for countless mercies bless Him
  Evermore and *now*.

The Dream of Athalie.

(FROM THE FRENCH OF RACINE.)

[ATHALIE or Athalia, worthy daughter of Ahab and Jezebel, having mas-
sacred all the children of Ahazia her son, excepting one named Joash,
who was hid in the temple, usurped the regal power. A dream troubles
her usurpation. She relates it to her chief minister and to Abner, general of her troops.]

A dream ! A dream ! Why should a dream me scare ?
Two unsubstantial figures in the air—
They follow me, they haunt me everywhere !

The first appeared to me at dead of night
In royal robes and all in queenly plight,
A settled majesty of proud disdain
Upon her marble features written plain :
" Daughter !" she said, " who from these breasts did
    draw
The drink of life when my least word was law."
" Daughter !" she said, " who on this neck hast hung,
Hath then that God his glamour o'er thee flung
Whom to oppose great Baal I did adore
In days of power that shall return no more,
Whom to resist hath been my being's aim ?
I pity thee that thine is not the same,
But like a craven culprit thou dost bow
Thy neck to yoke that it should never know."
Then as to embrace her I did try,

Naught but dead fragments could I there espy
Of bones, and flesh, and garments dyed in blood,
Limb torn from limb, and nothing that was good,
While gathering curs with hungry front teeth tore
The relics which a queen and mother wore !
From out the fragments rose a beauteous form
As if to quell a louring burst of storm,
A little figure clad in glittering white,
An angel in an amber sea of light,
But, strange to tell, close to it, on the air,
Glanced ever and anon a dagger bare.
He with firm grasp the dagger then did take
And still pursues me if I sleep or wake !
Once, in my fright, (which I could never scan,)
I to my mother's god for succour ran,
But Baalim heard not, answered not my prayer,
And all my cries were lost in empty air ;
Then to the Jewish Temple I did hie,
Where will not grief and fear make woman fly ?
I thought of offerings to appease the wrath
Of the Jews's God, yes, on my onward path
The people all made way, the sacrifice
Stopped for a time, but with affrighted eyes
I saw the very child I shunned, standing
By the high Priest, with an air commanding,
The very form and face and lips and hair ;
It was *reality*, no vision there,
Upon his young brow glanced a coronet,
He was a king, and yet no king as yet,
The people clapped, the trumpets blew right soon,
I trembled, reeled, and fell down in a swoon !

! L. of C.

Small Things.

A lone star at evening shineth
    With a dubious light on high,
But we see with deepening night-fall
    All the glories of the sky.

Near the hedge a small bird warbles,
    Warbles low and warbles long,
Then upon our rapt ears bursteth
    A full tide of choral song.

On the plant two tender blossoms,
    Green and sheathed, are seen to stand ;
Long before the magic circlets
    Into sunlit rays expand.

Pattering drops from heaven refresh
    April's thirsty sod and plain,
Months elapse—its flood-gates open
    And down comes the pouring rain.

Scorn not, Christian, days of small things,
    Weak beginnings though they be,
Tiny rills of crystal water
    Mingle with the vast blue sea.

The Inscription.

Stay, Heart, nor wander here and there
 By gusts of passion driven,
But lean upon the Friend who hath
 Thine iron fetters riven ;

And he shall teach thee how to feel,
 And how to overcome ;
Shall bind thy wounds, renew thy youth,
 And safely lead thee home ;

Shall form out of thee, stony heart,
 Now wandering about,
A pillar in the house of God
 That never stirreth out.

And a new name inscribe thereon
 In characters of light,
A name which to all eyes that read
 For ever be as bright !*

---

* "Him that overcometh will I make a pillar in the temple of my God, and he shall go no more out......and I will write upon him my new name." Rev. III. 12.

To "Arcydae."

(On reading his poem entitled the "Last Dream
of Life" in *Bengal Magazine*, No. 11.)

Is Ambition then thy last hope in this life,
Dear Arcydae! that lurid star whose light
Leads but to bogs and quicksands of this world.
Dost wish to die? to die and turn to dust?
Hast studied Shakespeare and rememberest
What he says? "In that sleep of death what dreams
May come—aye, there's the rub." Aye, there's the rub .
Say I once more. Your beckoning star may seem
A meteor-flash and ' burning thoughts' but scathe
And toss the soul in waves tumultuous ! But
If these things seem to thee as idle fears,
Chimeras of the brain, O yet believe
That for a higher, holier purpose than
That which you imagine, God gave thee being !
O believe that there is a heaven of bliss,
O believe that sin has marred the earth
And left its trail on every earthly thing
(That God makes all things perfect) O believe
That God is Love and watcheth o'er us all
And waiteth to redeem humanity
Of which *thou* art an unit. This is no
Maniac-world howling through the realms of space
In endless revolutions and mad zest,
But a nursery for God's own children.

The sky, the stars, the passion-panting sea,
The wide green earth, and all its store of flowers,
Are yet brimful of beauty, created
By His word, or, to express in language
More poetical, an emanation
From the light divine whence all things flow.
O believe there is a day when this light
Shall permeate all beings in full tide,
Creation's self shall clap its upraised hands,
Rock in golden undulations, and sing
For joy.   Each nook and crevice where darkness
Hideth shall be illumined.   Sin-shadows
Shall depart, and that direst shade of all,
The shade of death, shall reign no more.   God's throne
Be set on Earth.   And Earth hold jubilee
With the embracing heavens ! All is not lost
That seemeth to be lost while God doth live.

The New Year.

Smiles for the year that hath come in,
And tears for all the bygone years,
Too senseless he who holds it sin
To greet the NEW with smiles and tears.

O Past, we strow upon thy grave
The tribute, stem-dropt golden flowers ;
O Future, may we be as brave
As thou, who bravest us in sad hours.

Hard is ' the bivouac of life,'
May we to keep it be as strong ;
Glorious the issues of the strife,
Though fought with weary soul, and long.

Cheer up, faint soul, press onwards still,
Press through the woods to your own goal ;
See amber streaks are on the hill,
Press yonder and take heart, my soul.

There, when that Pisgah-height is reached,
Nor foes, nor darksome shades intrude,
In pure white light our garments bleached,
We worship the Eternal Good.

Epiphany.

The star! the star! the star!
His star is in the East,
A shimmering light,
On plain and height,
Proclaims the solemn feast.

The star! the star! the star!
Thy circlet never sets,
Thy soft gleam falls
On pagod walls,
And tops of minarets.

The star! the star! the star!
The Magi saw of yore;
What shall we bring
To our great King?
What hast thou, heart, in store?

The star! the star! the star!
All thoughts that in us stir,
Its glorious ray
Transmutes this day
To gold, and spice and myrrh.

The star! the star! the star!
Thou cloud-dispelling eye,
May the light roll
From soul to soul,
And angels hymn on High!

Hymn—Good Friday.

Sing, O my soul, for ever sing
The triumphs of my Saviour-King ;
He who did leave his throne above,
And He whose very name is Love ;
For me sin-lost the God-man came,
Died on the Cross the death of shame.

O Cross, O death, O bleeding side,
O Justice fully satisfied,
O Fount of blessing from which flows
The healing balm for all my woes,
O Lamb of God for sinners slain,
May I be Thine and Thine remain !

Easter.

Softly dawned the morning,
Cold winds were astir,
When the Maries hasted
To the Sepulchre.

Hearts in sorrow beating
For their buried Lord,
For the Master's accents,
For the Incarnate Word.

There a mighty Angel,
Clothed in spotless white,
With his lightning glances,
Met their aching sight.

And he told them, " Maries,
Fear not, Him ye seek
Is not here, but risen,
To His own bespeak."

As with joyous foot-steps
On their way they sail,
The Lord Himself appears
With the words " All hail."

Then they kneel and worship
Thee, the Risen One,
Light upon their garments
From the rising sun.

Each returning Easter
May we joy and pray,
Like to those two Maries
In that glorious day.

Ascension.

Let the sounding anthem swell,
    Christ hath triumphed
Over sin, and death, and hell :
        Hallelujah.

In a cloud of golden light
    Past the Saviour
Out of His own loved ones' sight :
        Hallelujah.

Now He sits at God's right hand,
    Sins forgiving,
Suppliants we before Him stand :
        Hallelujah.

Once again shall Olivet
    Be in a·glow,
When His throne on earth He'll set :
        Hallelujah.

All His saints with Him He'll bring
    In robes of light,
He Himself their crownèd King :
        Hallelujah.

A Carol.

It is the glorious Yuletide,
The birth-night of our King,
Let every heart be open
For joy and welcoming.
The chaste cold stars were throbbing
Upon the morning sky,
When bright-tiaraed angels
First raised the joyful cry—
" Glory to God, the highest,
On earth good-will to men"—
Should not that song be ringing
As even it rung then ?
Our King, the Lord of glory,
Our King, the Man forlorn,
Our King in heaven who reigneth,
Our King, the Virgin-born !
Our King, who gave His blessing
To them that did deride,
Our King o'er death triumphant,
Our King, the Crucified !

Another morn more glorious
Shall start into new birth,
When, o'er His foes victorious,
He sets His throne on earth.
Another song of triumph
Shall rise with loud acclaim,
When learneth every nation
The Great Mashiach's name.
A loftier diapason,
A holier song of praise,
Than sang those shining angels
In old Judean days !

Sweet Replies.

1

I am sick, Lord Christ, sharp pains I feel ;—
" The Great Healer I, and I shall heal."

2

I am poor, Lord Christ, all day I pine ;—
" I will enrich, for true wealth is mine."

3

I am bound, Lord Christ, as you well see ;—
" I will break thy bands and set thee free."

4

I'm worldly, and I am hard of heart ;—
" I'll teach thee to choose the better part."

5

Snivelling and sad the tones of my voice ;
" In me thou shalt aye truly rejoice."

6

This skin is noisome, and leprous, and sore ;—
" One touch of mine shall its bloom restore."

7

I'm slothful and therefore fail to come ;—
" I seek the strayed ones and bring them home."

8

I stifle oft the grace you bestow ;—
" God's gift never repentance doth know."

9

Nor pore o'er Thy Book from day to day ;—
" But still each moment you've power to pray."

10

Good Lord ! Every doubting plea you've waived ;—
" Believe in me and thou shalt be saved."*

---

* See Goodwyn's " Child of Light," a most excellent treatise on Christian experience. These old Puritans were true men of God.

Verses.

Yes, I meet you loved ones often
 Though the seas between us roll,
Every morning, at heaven's portal,
 Every evening, soul meets soul.

Worldlings cannot guess the meaning
 Of our hidden life and love,
For they know not how in absence
 We have power to meet above.

Children of a loving Father,
 By the broad high road of prayer
We rejoice in His blest presence
 Every time we gather there.

In those palace halls and gardens
 Often yet we sing and play,
There we find dear ones departed,
 In those realms of endless day.

There beside the sparkling river
 Where the sun-light crisply falls,
And the budding creepers mantle
 Over jasper-gleaming walls.

There where stands in bloom perpetual
 The Life-tree with healing leaves,
And the lawn its scented white flowers,
 Jocund on her lap receives.

May we play as now we often
 Play at morn or close of day,
Play and bless our loving Father
 In that long, long holiday.

A Colloquy with the Evening Star.

(ABOUT CHRIST'S MIGHTY LOVE.)

How goes the world O star?
" In its old accustomed way,—
  Some laugh, some weep, some fail, some win,
  All triumph in their sin,
  Thus day succeedeth day."

Is there then hope for man?
" Yea, hope steadfast, sure and true ;
  Yon western clouds, bright gates of gold,
  Through them you may behold
  Heaven's soft cerulean blue."

Is it all peace in heaven?
" Neither sin nor sorrow there,
  Jesus, the King, calls all his saints
  To leave the old earth's taints
  His bliss with Him to share."

"Together let us sing"
  The star said on—" His love,
  A plaintive, soft duet—till slow
  All voices join below
  All voices join above"!

Millenial Hymn.

(*For India.*)

Ye mountains crowned with hoar-frost,
Ye rivers welling strong,
And bursting on the plains below,
First raise the glorious song.
Ye forests with dark-shadowing trees,
Ye fields of golden grain,
Ye grots and caverns, heights and flats,
Sound back the joyous strain.

Ye beasts of royal prowess,
Ye birds of hundred dyes,
Ye blushing fruits, Ye bursting flowers,
Wake up with startled eyes ;
Wake up and join the hymn of praise,
Of gratitude and love,
To Him who sits at God's right hand,
The Christ who rules above.

The song is raised, O people,
That Christ will come again ;
That Christ will come in majesty
Upon the earth to reign.
Long pent in superstition's night,
Enslavèd though ye be
By sin and sin's dominion,
Yet He shall make you free.

Shout ye that song of triumph
In each differing tongue,
Be numbered with the nations
That shall to Him belong :
Thus shall the Sun of Righteousness
Chase all dark shades away,
And India bask beneath the light
Of never-ending day.

To Macleod Wylie, Esq.,

For thee, for thee, the starry wreath
  That decks the evening sky,
For thee, for thee, the azure flowers
  Upon the hill-tops high.

For thee, for thee, the silent sea
  With all its wealth of shells,
For thee, for thee, the Druid oak,
  Or those soft minster bells.

For thee, for thee, a solitude
  By kindly Nature sent,
To gather patience for thy work
  And hoard a life-content.

For thee, for thee, Religion's light
  Undimmed by priestly saw,
A flowing tide from God Himself,
  A tide of love and awe.

For thee, for thee, the *mind* that makes
  The poet and the sage,
Who leaves to nations yet unborn
  The impress of his age.

To my boy 10 years old,

Pray and study—plan and work
Thou little Bezaleel !
Life's morning is the time to put
Thy shoulder to the wheel.

Carve the timber, cut the stone
And work in brass and gold,
And let the decorations be
Devised in fairest mould.

Search and find within thy soul
What unwrought riches lie ;
Love, joy, and precious truthfulness,
A hidden treasury.

Search and find within that Book
What gems divine, whose ray
A lamp unto thy feet shall be
And lighten all thy way.

Daily, hourly, toil abroad,
The heart has wide domains,
Waiting culture, flag not, fear not,
Though there be drought and rains.

Build a palace beautiful
Enchased below, above,
That when the Master-worker comes
He may thy work approve !

To my Children.

Children ! there's a better glass
Than that in which you see the face
Every morning when you rise,
Can you tell me where it lies ?
It lies where the green alders grow,
A mirror true for all who go,
Of large dimensions, silver-bright,
And gleaming in the sun's pure light.

Children ! there are better flowers
Than in those dresses prized of yours,
Those trickt flounces, and that plume,
Beside them placed, poor looks assume.
Roses, kingcups, blue-bells, daisies,
Nature whom the poet praises,
Has such embroidered satins rare,
With them your garbs hold no compare.

Children ! there is better food
To be found in heath and wood
Than what is on the table set
Before you, cream or omelet.
The mountain-breeze, the fresh, the free,
That wanders over earth and sea
Is it not sweeter than this wine?
Is it not food and drink divine?

Children ! there's a better home,
Not made of bricks or painted loam,
Not decked with pictures on the wall,
That shall never crumbling fall ;
A home, beyond the azure skies,
Of many mansions, there to rise
Should be our aim, yes, there above,
We shall know our Father's love.

Child's Morning Hymn.

Sweet as from each flower-cup
The incense riseth up
In this hour of morning,
Sweet be my thoughts of Thee.

Bright as the sun now shines
And clouds with amber lines
On his triumphant wake,
Bright be my thoughts of Thee.

Loud as the song-birds' chaunt
From cage and bushy haunt,
Pouring their hymns of praise,
Loud be my thoughts of Thee.

To Thee I consecrate
Once more myself, and wait
To know Thy blessed will,
My Father and my God !

Child's Evening Hymn.

Yes, all the sun-lit hours have flown,
All my appointed work is done,
And here alone I kneel and pray,
As twilight ends another day,
Oh ! Father, listen to the cry
Of weak and trusting Infancy.

Thine is the bending arch of blue,
The earth and all its treasures too,
Its trees, its flowers, its light, its air,—
Thy love is scattered everywhere,
Where'er I turn my eyes I see
The impress of Divinity.

The birds, that far for food did roam,
Now hasten to their wood-land home,
The bee that all day long did strive
To gather honey,—seeks the hive,
And, like the winged bird and bee,
My weary soul seeks rest in Thee.

Lord ! make me loving, gentle, mild
As Jesus thy belovèd child ;
Keep me, when night deep slumber brings,
Under the shadow of Thy wings,
So shall I in thy love rejoice
And praise Thee with my heart and voice.

Hymn.

What though my sins in order stand
As countless as the ocean-sand,
What though the leprosy is seen
On tongue and lips and hands and mien ;
Though all is dark and vile within,
Doubt and despair and deadly sin,
In that great day—this is my plea
That Thou, O Lord, hast died for me !

Not what I can or cannot do
Will aught avail, O Tried and True!
For long before this fleeting breath
Was called to being, by Thy death
Heaven had been won, the ransom paid,
For sin a full atonement made ;
What though the vilest vile I be,
Is not Thy *finished work* my plea ?

Clothed in that robe, at Thy right hand,
Redeemed by Thee, Thine own shall stand ;
On earth the great white throne be spread,
And all the graves give up their dead ;
The awful book be opened wide,
The Son of Man shall then decide,
And He shall rule—blest be His name !
With two-edged sword and eyes of flame.

Hymn.

No fountain issuing from the rock can purer water give
Than that which comes from Thee, my Lord, which let me
    drink and live.
The fountain runs 'neath shade and sun and dark or bright
    may be,
But Thou remainest same alway, there is no change in Thee.

" My soul panteth after God as the hart for water-brook"
In faith sang Judah's warrior-king, in faith for Thee did
    look.
And when on earth Thou walk'dst 'mong men,— from
    bondage to set free,
To every fainting soul there came,—Thy thrice-blest " Come
    to Me."

And once again when from God's throne the crystal stream
    shall flow,
And the famed city like a bride in all its beauty glow,
Then louder than the golden harps in that our long lost
    home,
The Spirit and the bride shall say,—to all athirst—" O
    Come !"

Hymn.

Oh wondrous love! oh wondrous power!
    To feel Thy presence from this hour;
Siloam's stream—where is it now?
    We know not—but we know that Thou
Art God and Love, to Thee we pray,
Thy blood can cleanse all sins away.

Blind from my birth—aye, doubly blind!
    To Thee I come my way to find,
Thou art the Way, the Truth, the Light,
    Oh! cleanse my soul—oh heal my sight;
That from all other gods set free
I may *in spirit* worship Thee!

Xmas.

Around the green-stemmed Christmas tree,
Bright, pendulous with fruits and flowers,
We'll celebrate the Saviour's birth,
And thus enjoy the precious hours.

The taper-lights and glistening balls
Shall shine like the pure stars above,
And as the Angels sing in heaven,
We too shall sing " we love, we love."

We'll sing and pray that this fair tree,
Meet emblem of the tree of life,
May scatter blessings far and near,
Renew all hearts and heal all strife.

Exotic blest ! deep may thy stem
Strike root in every heathen sod,
Till turning from their idols dumb
All peoples know to worship God.

Hymn.

Thou art our true Gilgal—in Thee, dear Lord,
Egypt's reproach has clean been swept away ;
The plague of darkness that hung o'er our soul
Is gone—Thou turnest darkness into day.

In Thee is stored the old corn of the land,
The light and love of God—on Thee we feed ;
The manna-showers of Law are now no more,
In Thee we find all that our spirits need.

With Thee dark Jordan's flood we've safely past,
O circumcise our hearts and make them Thine ;
What further fights there may be, lead Thou on,
Till Canaan's promised land before us shine.

Two Thoughts.

The poet thinks—
" For forms of Faith, let priests and zealots fight,
His can't be wrong whose life is in the right."

I think—
Life *may* be wrong, sin *may* be strong, but yet
Souls trusting in the Lord salvation get,
For *forms* to fight is but a paltry thing,
But glorious is the fight for Christ our King.
This fight is not with weapons like the sword,
But by my Spirit saith the blessed Lord.

The Church.

The world is a toy-box with broken lid
Fit for the burning—in which is hid
A Pearl of rarest price, concocted—where ?
In ocean, earth, or in the realms of air ?*
Not in such places did it being find,
But in the pure depths of the Eternal mind,
Love was the root, LOVE bore for it the Cross,
To spill life-blood LOVE counted it no loss,
So when LOVE found it, LOVE sold *all* he had
With that ONE PEARL, LOVE was so very glad.

---

* Hindu tradition has it that pearls drop like rain-drops.

POEMS.—INDIAN.

Introduction.

WE have many histories of India, from school-histories up to elaborate treatises, but no work embodying Indian historical incidents and characters and older traditions in a poetical form. Yet India is truly the land of romance and poetry, whether we direct our attention to the varied beauty and magnificence of its natural features, or to the wonderful incidents of its earliest and later annals. Where on the whole earth can be found a country displaying the sublime and the lovely as on a stage, and all the wealth of the frigid, the temperate, and torrid zones, as in a bazaar? From the lofty Himalayas crowned with eternal snows to the flat plains of Bengal waving with green crops, from Dera Gazee Khan to Trivandrum, the scenery is as varied as it is possible to imagine. Where again are such flowers as are to be seen in India? Where such fruits? Where such exuberance of foliage, where such rivers, quadrupeds, song-birds? Turning to its history we find in those gigantic epics, the Rámáyána and Máhàbharata, such an inexhaustible mine of the romantic and poetical, and to its later history such stirring incidents, such oriental gorgeousness, such rapid rise and extinction of dynasties, such a marvellous development of the plans of Divine Providence, that neither the poet nor the romancer can be at a loss for subjects to write upon. The author of this little volume does not pretend to the gifts and qualifications which constitute either, and can only hope that some one will do for Indian history what Lord Macaulay has done for the history of old Rome, or Lockhart has done for ancient Spanish legends in his beautiful Ballads. All that he has

attempted to do is to versify or put into metre certain passages in the history of India, arranging them in chronological
order ; and as metrical compositions exercise a more powerful
influence than prose, especially on the young, he trusts his
attempts will not be altogether without use.   Waving therefore all claims to poetic excellence for these fugitive poems,
it is no presumption to state that those marked " From the
Sanscrit," though not all close translations, have been written
with as becoming reverence to the spirit and tone of the ori-
ginals as their transfusion into a foreign tongue, and into
some of the most approved metres of modern English Poetry
would admit, and those marked " From Indian history," are
genuine scenes and events as the pages of history will testify.
It is in the meagreness of the author's powers, and not in the
meagreness of the subjects, that the short-comings and de-
fects of the work rest.   The history of India appropri-
ately divides itself into three distinct periods, the Hindoo
period, the Muhammedan period, and the British period.
The poems refer only to the two first.   The British period,
though replete with subjects, has not been touched upon at all,
belonging as it does to times comparatively modern.   That
wonderful concatenation of events which led to the rise of the
British power in India, which converted a factory in Surat
into an empire mightier, vaster, than that over which the eagle
of all-conquering Rome ever flew, is in itself a Romance which
justifies the observation that " truth is stranger than fiction."
The abolition of cruel rites, the spread of education and
enlightenment, the ushering in of a new era, as it were, in
India's cycle of humanity, and one may say of its nationality,
all through the divinely selected instrument of British power
or domination, open wide fields for the display of genuine

authorship. Up, up, up, in the regions of poesy and grateful song live the remembrances of such administrative measures as the abolition of the Suttee-rite and other barbarities sanctioned by India's debasing idolatry. How interesting again would be a novel penned with the picturesque gorgeousness of the author of " Rienzi," or the powerful touches of the authoress of " Jane Eyre," describing the experiences of the educated young Indian or the trials and hopes of the Convert brought out of darkness into light. But all this in due time and by men worthy of the task. We have never thought it beyond hope that under the benign British sway Indians will be able to frame and fashion a National Literature of their own, not in Hindustani, or Bengali, or Mahratti, or Tamil, or Telugu, or Urya, but in the English language. All the beautiful literature of America is of recent date. And though Indians do not exactly bear the same relationship as Americans (so-called) to the mother-country, yet the time may come for her to boast that her fostering care has called out in the land of her adoption—poets, romancers, philosophers. There is hope for all this in the common Aryan origin of the people of England and India.

The Magic Fawn.

(From the Sanscrit.)

Far hid amid that wilderness of gloom the forest Dandaka
Lay the lovely valley, lit up by the sun's golden radiance,
Like beauty imprisoned in some sombrous castle yet cheerful!
A river watered the valley, and on its dallying wavelets
White lotuses gleamed, half open, nectar-cups for the wild-
    swan,
And on the green margin, with colors like those of the rain-
    bow,
Flowers spread their tender petals. The feathery Acacia
And the red-blossomed Simaltree grew on the higher undul-
    ations.
Like heroes guarding the vale stood the palms in fitful
    clusters
Lit up at eve by innumerable troops of fire-flies.
The Baubool with gleaming fruits formed a stately throne for
    the peacock,
Who, as the clouds rumbled, spread his tail with golden stars
    bestudded.
Bees and butterflies roamed here and there, and afar in the
    distance,
Shaded by plantain-leaves, was the hut of the exile brothers.
Tendrils of creepers hung from the eaves, and often the song-
    birds
Came there to pour out their little souls in mellifluous music,

Or peck grains from the rosy palm of the beautiful Sita.
Thus stood that humble dwelling of joy in rural seclusion
Enclosed by the forest Dandaka with huge trees, dark alleys,
Rank grass and moaning wind, the abode of the wicked
    Rakhasas.

One morn when birds were awake and singing, and the slant
    sun-beams
Were drinking the liquid ambrosia that lay in the flower-bells,
And the breezes of summer were beginning to play on the
    grasses,
At the door of the hermitage stood that woman of women
The beautiful Sita, happy in banishment, thinking perchance
Of by-gone days and Aoudhya : when lo ! from the thicket
That bounded the landscape on one of its sides, out-darted
A radiant fawn ! Its small horns of gold tipped with
    diamonds,
Eyes brighter than rubies and skin like the crystal shining ;
Amethyst bells hung from a tie round its neck, each bell-tongue
    a pearl,
And their tintinabulation was something so exquisite,
Something so like the music which she loved to hear in her
    childhood,
That it charmed her whole being to joy! To Rama she
    hastens
And says, " Get me, my Rama, this prize, I, who ne'er ask
    you for aught,
Ask for this dear gazelle !" Lakhshmana o'erheard, and with
    sage counsel
Thus accosted the queen, " No fawn, dear Sita, can thus be
    arrayed,

'Tis some Rakhasa disguised." But she would not listen ;
    and Rama,
Loth to refuse his beloved, with quiver and bow forth sallied ;
" Guard," he said to Lakhshmana, " brother, guard her while
    I am away,
I have nothing to fear e'en though it be the king of Rakhasas.

To capture the fawn alive was Rama's aim, but it eluded
His coaxing and efforts ; at length over the dew-spangled
    grasses
He gave it full chase, and the beautiful creature ran panting
Now hither now thither, with such desperate bounds, at times
    hiding
Behind some furze-bush, then leaping o'er streamlets which
    gurgled
From the sides of the hills, till it reached the dark forest
    Dandaka,
That he felt sure in his mind it was some malevolent demon.
Onwards he followed it, as nothing could daunt the Invincible,
Nor shades which for ever lour nor trees which for ever are
    wailing :
Then stringing his lordly bow, the gift of the sage Viswamitra,
He from his bundle of white-feathered darts selected the
    keenest
And discharged it amain. The fawn fell with a cry which
    resounded
Through those dim shades for leagues, a cry for help in a
    voice like Rama's,
And Rama beheld at his feet the dying demon Maritcha.
Thus, even in death, the wicked cease not from treacherous
    devices.

With louder wailing now wailed the trees of the forest
Dandaka,
The sky scarcely seen through the old creaking branches, was
beclouded,
A raven that with prying eyes on the bloody spot alighted
Flew back in a flutter, singing hoarsely the demon's requiem,
The demon Maritcha slain by the death-fraught arrow of
Rama.

Meanwhile the cry had reached the ears of the tender-hearted
Sita,
Who said, " Hie thee, Lakhshmana, Rama calleth for help ;"
but Lakhshmana
Well knew it was a cry to deceive, some plan, some desperate
attempt
To draw him out and thus leave his lovely sister protector-less :
So he gave vent to his thoughts, " No beautiful queen of
Aoudhya,
No honored Sita, that is not Rama's voice, the Invincible
Can ne'er need a protector, ne'er call for another's assistance,
If I leave you alone I fear some evil of import may happen,
My mind this morn is uneasy and full of direful fore-bodings :"
Wrathful, anxious, and with eyes swimming in tears the
other replied
" Think'st thou, Lakhshmana, that I can mistake the voice
of my lord, my husband,
Think'st thou I would request you to go without weighty
occasion,
Many thanks, young hero, I know not about what you are
dreaming,
Is it my hand when Rama is dead, or the throne of Aoudhya" ?

Lakhshmana looking up—his honor thus strangely derided,
Said softly, " O woman-soul! unjust and ungenerous ever,
I go, but here I draw a strong line with the point of my
    arrow,
Step not beyond it, it is a magic line, and will guard you
    from ill."
With these words he left the hermitage in quest of his
    brother,
And Sita wept and mused, mused and wept at the hut-thresh-
    hold alone !

Now over the sky's stony pavement the red sun was galloping
And the air and the earth the light of his bright flag-roll
    reflected,
Sita still stood at the door, and on the scene appeared
    another,
An old man, clothed in rags, creeping it seemed that way to
    his homestead,
He approached leaning upon his staff and· mumbling
    inaudibly,
Then as his eyes met her's distinctly pronounced the word
    " Alms."
Sita, ever anxious to help or soothe the poor and afflicted,
Ran in and returned with a large measure of rice in a basket
And offered it kindly, but the stranger, who was standing
    beyond
The line drawn by Lakhshmana, drew not nearer, but thus
    accosted,
" What boots it, fair ladye, to fear an old man like me, a
    beggar,
A doubting heart and a willing hand are signs of uncharity

Which a ladye like thee should shun, am I a beast of the
    forest,

Or a leper, that thus you should keep aloof ? Nay, ladye I go

Without accepting your gift." At these words Sita some-
    what abashed

Stepped out of the magic line. On a sudden the stranger
    vanished,

And in his stead, looming athwart the sun, stood the tall dark
    figure

Of the king of Rakhasas, Maritcha's friend, ten-headed Ravan ;

Shriek after shriek burst from the affrighted Sita as quick he
    hurled

Her into his car, with wheels strong as thunder, drawn by
    Pisachas.

Mandodari.

(From the Sanscrit.)

It was a lofty palace-hall,
 The pillars marble-white,
Festooned with mimic flowers, upheld
 A dome of chrysolite.
High in the centre hung the orbèd moon.
At every niche stood silver trees
 With leaves of curious mould,
And on the glittering boughs
 Were birds of gold.
 While here and there
Jets springing fell in star-showers,
 A fragrance filled the air.
By some magic power those birds sang sweetly.
 But the old grey sea
Breaking on coral-reefs, and wafting spicy gales,
Made meeter music for Mandodari.

Eyes down-dropt and pencilled with dark brows,
Eyes in which shone the light of chastity,
Lips severe as beseem a queen,
 And tresses flowing free
 Over the span-broad zone,
These were thine, regal Mandodari !

For thee all seasons brought their dower,—
Spring its spray-wreath and opening flower,
Summer its golden-rinded fruit,
And mellow Autumn its rich treasure-store ;
For thee the deep gave shining shells
 Big with twin-pearls,
For thee the mine was made to yield
 Its burning ore.

R.

Queen of the monarch with ten crowns
At whose name the immortals trembled !
Thy soul-full eyes, thy ambrosial smile
Could the tyrant's heart beguile
        And subdue his frowns.
Yet fearful that he may not yield,
Thou didst devise that royal game
In which a battle strong is fought
Upon a mimic battle-field.*

Queen of the monarch with ten crowns,
        Queen, but not happy !
Not thus were spent thy childhood's days
        At thy royal father's home,
For there in maiden-freedom thou didst roam
O'er field and lawn and sun-lit ways ;
Fed with the honey culled by yellow bees
        From the forest's flowering trees,
And resting on beds of eider-down,
The apple of thy mother's eye,
Thou worshiptst the white form of virgin purity.

But ah ! the change, I see thee stand
At the gorgeous palace-window,
Thy sad brow resting on thy hand Mandodari !
Think'st thou of those bright days for ever gone
Of thy false lord or of thy warrior son Mandodari ?
Or think'st thou of thine own tender mother
        So loving who was to thee,
Or listless watchest tumbling foam-balls,
        Gazing on the sea ?
Never fell on queen or maiden,
Though the earth be sorrow-laden,
        Such sad destiny !

---

* Mandodari, Ravan's queen, is said to have invented the game of chess.

Jatayu.

(*From the Sanscrit.*)

High upon his rocky eyrie
    Sat Jatayu, royal bird !
On the tree-tops of the forest
    Not a breeze the leaflets stirred ;
But the sun with lingering radiance
    Gilded that broad sea of green,
And the shadows of the mountains
    Slept like giant-forms between.

Gazing still and idly gazing
    On the fiery sun-set's glow
Sate he, thinking of some on-slaught
    In elk-haunted glades below,
Or of mounting on swift pinions
    Higher up the ether blue,
Till the earth is dim and speck-like
    And heaven's portals start to view.

Hark ! what distant sound of wailing
    Rings across the leaden sky,
On the air a whirling chariot
    Drawn by fiery horses fly.
King Jatayu saw and knew it,
    Clapped his wings and raised his crown ;
From his proud throne on the mountain
    Like dark thunder swooped a-down.

First he swooped upon the horses
    Left them gasping on the plain,

Then the monster's heavy javelins
   Fell as thick as hail or rain ;
Nothing daunted, wildy wheeling
   Near the spot where Ravan stood,
Dashed his chariot into fragments,
   Rolling fragments marked with blood.

Two black wings from earth uprising
   Carried Ravan on his way,
But the Vulture-King pursues him
   Set to fight the desp'rate fray.
" Save me, save me, good Jatayu,"
   Sita, best of women, cried,
As with firmer grasp the Demon
   Held her by the hair in pride.

Now with beak and claws assailing
   Ravan's twenty eyes he gored,
Who in anger fiercely yelling
   Drew at once his magic sword.
Thrice three times the flashing weapon
   Missed its ill-directed aim,
Then upon Jatayu's pinion
   Fell as falls the lightning-flame.

Like a soldier slain in battle
   Lies Jatayu on the strand,
From his throat the red blood welling
   Mixes with the ' glinting' sand ;
And the death-film slowly gathers
   In his bright, sun-loving eyes,
As he lived a mountain-hero,
   So a hero's death he dies !

The Aerial Journey of Rama and his Consort.

(From the Sanscrit.)

High into air the heavenly chariot rose ;
(Bearing within that doubly precious freight
Ayoudha's king and queen ;) at intervals
It hung beneath some cloud from which the light
Fell in long spikes upon its rounded top,
Or glanced upon the silver bells that made
Incessant music ; but at other times
Fast it sailed, sun-clad, clearing league on league,
Like some strong bird that sails with wings outspread.
As they passed o'er the borders of the sea
Rama addressed his tender-hearted spouse,

" Mark, love, the sea slow opens to the view
Its dark waves decked with foam. The roseate sky
Is pictured in those depths where once of old
The sage Kapila from our fathers hid
The Sacrificial Steed of prowess rare ;
The sun with beams of power drinks its salt waves,
And on the eve primeval, rose the moon
From its fair surface.   Gems of every hue
Illume its secret caves and grow with time.
A limitless expanse ! Meand'ring rills,
Like maidens coy in varied vestment clad
Are by its waters courted and embraced ;
Amid the foam-flakes float and disappear
Serpents with jewelled crowns and sparkling scales,

And that huge beast, the monarch of the sea,
High on the air throws up a sheeny shower.
Upon the shore the sands are strewn with pearls
And white as white can be.   The wanton breeze
Which, as we veer, blows full upon your face,
Bears on its wings the breath and dust of flowers
On coral rocks that blow.   A column dense
Of multiplying clouds invests the eastern sky,
And as Mount Mandar glowed when the leagued gods
With it the ocean churned, so glows the mass
Lit by the radiance of departing day.
Lo ! On the dim horizon's farthest verge
The tall *tamalas* to the eye appear
Like weeds of stunted growth, and yonder range
Of slender betel-nuts, a border rare.
All behind, seem following our bright car,
And when you stretch your fair hand to the clouds
The lightning decks it like some ornament :—
The pious hermits of Yanasthana
New huts are building.   Here it was I found
(When mad in quest of you) a priceless treasure,
String'd jewels of your feet, dropped in your haste.
Those trees with their green arms and greener leaves
Did direct my way, and with lifted eyes
Yon browsing antelopes partook my grief.
Mark there, the summit of Malcaban mount
Sky-piercing, rock on rock of adamant ;
While passing by its base, so sweet the scent
Kadamba flowers exhaled, and so plaintive
Was the peacock's cry, and so musical
The voice of clouds resounding from its caves,

Absence from thee was more than ever felt.
On the adjoining lake I saw the swans
Pass lotus-leaves from bill to bill, and clasped
The young *asoke* that overhung its steeps
Loaded with flowers, meet emblem of thy beauty.
As pass we on, the car's silvery bells
Put yonder line of storks upon the wing ;
And here, O ' dainty-waisted' ! is the grove
Half of whose trees were watered by your hands.
The wild stags in its shades are gazing up.
Here on Godavery's flower-enamelled banks
Of old I rested, on your lap my head,
When tired of chasing the quick-bounding roe ;
The time comes back as it were yesterday!
Here dwells the sage austere, Agastya named,
Who in the height of blazing summer's heat
Amid four flaming fires abstracted prays ;
And there another of a different mind
Whose life luxurious is a round of joys ;
Yon pleasure-dome hemmed in by waters clear,
And glistening through embowering leaves, is his,
In its bright halls the flower-crowned *apsaras*
Or lead the merry dance or sing sweet songs.
Hark, even now at intervals I hear
Such soul-subduing strains from pipe, and lute,
And dulcimer, as ne'er I heard before.
Now is the lofty peak of Cheetrakute
Dimly descried.   From it serenely flows
Mandakni, queen of rills, and like a string
Of pearls adorns the landscape clothed in green.
Far, far, in front behold bright steps of light

Our journey's end, and at their base the troops
Of pluméd soldiers that attend with flags
Emblazoned, fluttering in the wind, and shields
Of gold, and gleaming spears, and instruments
Of martial music, to receive their king.
Surrounded by his ministers of state,
A hero with a hero's form and mien,
There stands the regent, my loving brother,
Impatient to give back the crown he wears.
Under the youth's just sway the kingdom rests
In peace, the subjects are as happy
As ever those of wisest lord that ruled."

The Bridal of Draupadee.

PART I.

(From the Sanscrit.)

The moon shines faint, the stars are few
That deck Yamuna's waves of blue,
The wild kokil has ceased to sing,
Hushed is the bee's soft murmuring,
The breeze that sighs around the bowers
Bears on its wings the breath of flowers
That sleep beneath the pale moon-beam,
And stirs no ripplet in the stream.
And naught disturbs, nor voice, nor sound,
The silence sad that reigns around.
The maidens of Vrij no longer play
'Neath the brown shade of creepers gay,
No longer is heard their song so sweet,
Nor the musical tread of their glancing feet,
Nor the lute of the god whose vestments shine
With the choicest stores of the brook and mine,
Whose locks with peacock-plumes are crowned,
Whose wrists with rings of gold are bound,
Whose dark-blue throat bright gems illume
Like stars that gleam through evening's gloom.
He is gone from the bowers of pleasure and love
To Indra's emerald realms above,
For the lord of the sky implores his aid
To prosper the love of a dark-browed maid.

The bridal hall was hung with flowers
Culled from Panchala's lakes and bowers,

There, lotuses in rich array
In garlands hung—like stars of day,
The *champac* in its golden bloom
Shone, and exhaled a rich perfume,
The sunflower with its circling beams
Recalled the lover's noon-tide dreams,
Nor were there wanting those fair gems,
The modest pride of other stems,
Kadamba 'neath whose checkered shade
The amorous Krishna danced and played,
And *vakul* prince of flowering trees
Home of sweet-warbling birds and bees,
And *bela* with its buds of white
Like manna-showers in vases bright,
Asoka too whose tender shoot
Blossoms when touched by maiden's foot,
With these, and more, that princely hall
Was ready dight to welcome all.
Sounded the conch-shell—and the bride,
With two fair maidens at her side,
Now sallied forth, in jewel's sheen,
At once of Love and Beauty queen !
Dark are her locks and dark her eyes—
A virgin daughter of the skies !
Her lips are redder than coral can be,
Her form more soft than the Simal tree,
And Oh ! when she moves 'tis with greater grace
Than the gliding swan on the still tank's face.

The youthful princes hied amain
O'er upland height, far stretching plain,

Each from his mansion and domain.
Again the conch-shell gaily sounds !
A league's length from the palace-bounds
The Target-fish hung high in air
From poles festooned with garlands rare,
And on each side the dais was spread
Sashes and shawls hung overhead
For awning, the empurpled light
Mocked many fluttering streamers white.
The citizens in groups advance
Armed with sword, javelin, or lance ;
The trumpets speak and horses prance.
Maskers and mimics too are there
In motley dresses quaint and rare,
And minstrel-bards, and women's eyes
Watching who wins the lovely prize,
And wrestlers famous in the ring
To shew their feats before the king,
And children shouting as one falls,
And gew-gaw sellers in their stalls,
And dancers in their beauty's pride
And knots of gypsies, eager-eyed !
Anon, as music swells the breeze,
Forth issuing from a screen of trees
The royal train appears—the sun
Its jocund course had nearly run,
Its last faint rays of crimson hue
Glanced on those spears and caftans blue,
And cloth of gold, and pennons high,
And all that glorious company !
On moved the pageant, clearer still

The trumpet-echoes from yon hill,
The drums resound, the chargers neigh
As if to meet a coming fray,
And elephants in trappings red,
By touch of steel-goad on the head
Are guided, on each back of power
A jewelled room as lady's bower ;
Who now can fitly paint or say
The glories of that bridal day ?
All souls seemed happy—happiest he
Who wins the far-famed Draupadee !

PART II

As one by one the princes try
The appointed feat of archery
To prove their skill—the crowds huzza
And nearer in a circle draw,
But all their rising zest expire
At ill success—they flag, retire.
Each suitor with his head bent low
Eyes resting on the vase below
Of limpid water picturing bright
The Target-fish (which danced in light)
Must send through five concentric rings
An arrow quivering on its wings
Straight to its destined goal. But, lo !
Some even fail to bend the bow,
So hard the wood, so tough the string,
The archer to the ground they fling,
Thus bravely wrought by king's command
To try the noblest of the land.

From proud Hastina's royal tower,
Where Dhritarashtra reigned in power,
His hundred sons had hastened, men
Whose like we ne'er shall see again,
(From swart Duryodhun, eldest-born,
To faces young and fair as morn,)
With beating heart each bent the bow,
Whose the bride-prize none yet may know ;
But as each prince in turn did fail,
The crowds began to smile and rail,

And Drona inly groaned with rage,
Drona, the warrior and the sage,
Whose darts, they say, were wing'd with flame,
Ne'er swerved aside, ne'er missed their aim,
And at whose famous martial-school
Those youths had learnt by book and rule.

But where amid that throng is he
The pride of India's chivalry?
The envy of Hastina's lord,
Matchless alike with bow or sword,
The soldier tried, the lover true,
Sure love for love was but his due,
The favored of the gods, and blest,
Why is he not among the rest?
In Brahmin's guise young Arjun stands
Amid the pressing soldier-bands.
With modest mien the bow he took,
The maidens whispered, others shook
Their heads, as much to say, restrain
Young man thy daring, 'tis in vain.
With one thought to the gods above
Another on his ladye-love
He strung the bow, and the suspense
And silence were in truth intense,
The arrow hurtled in the sky
And struck the Fish triumphantly,
The image in the waters clear
Seemed rent in twain to standers near.
And forthwith in a fragrant shower
From Indra's heaven fell bud and flower.

Now sound the bridal-note with glee,
For Arjun's wife is Draupadee !
Let silver-fife and rolling drum
Keep pace with the increasing hum
Of men and women, on the air
Which seemed a roseate tint to bear ;
For Indra had so touched the light
That it became both red and bright :
From his own heaven he sent a ray
At evening, on that gala-day.
But soon confusion filled the scene
And battle stained the bridal-green,
The Kuru princes sought a fray,
With armèd men they lined the way,
And glittering spears told every one
Of fight for her who had been won.
Duryodhun led the first fierce band,
The other owned Kurna's command,
A valiant leader true and tried,
To Dhritarashtra's cause allied.
What were the brothers now to do,
Their hands unarmed, their men so few ?
Arjun snatched up and strung the bow,
To Kurna sent a cleaving blow ;
And Bhima tearing up a tree
Whirled round his head as fierce and free ;
Their followers few like lions fought
And turned the opposing lines to naught ;
The favor of the gods on high
Secured a signal victory.

Again in Gokul's spicy grove
Breeze, bird, and bee, in gladness rove,
And at the soft approach of Spring
The trees and plants are blossoming.
Again upon the emerald green
Is heard the lute, the dance is seen ;
Again Yamuna's waves of blue
Are rippling in the moonlight new ·
Which shining brightly seem to say
To jocund hearts, keep holiday,
For Krishna from the realms above
Hath hied back to his bowers of love.

Autumn.

(From the Sanscrit.)

In garbs of white and decked with flowers
Fair Autumn comes to bless our bowers ;
Moves she with unstudied grace,
Mellow lustre on her face,
Along her path flowers spring and bloom
And load the air with rich perfume,
And songs of birds seem music sweet
From rings gem-set that bind her feet.

Gently flow the maiden streams
'Neath the moon's unshaded beams,
And fishes glancing in the light
Make the wavelets yet more bright,
Upon their trembling waters now
Lotuses in numbers blow,
And like white garlands hung on air
The herons deck their bosoms fair.
No clouds are on the vasty sky
Save its own robes of royalty,
Which here are wrought with living gold,
And there, white tints and streaks unfold,
The dimpling rills, earth, air, and sky,
Raise youthful hearts to ecstacy.

O'er the broad plain and on the hill
Night's dusky gleam is lingering still,
And the wind with dew-drops laden
Pains and grieves the love-lorn maiden,
While from lotus' cups it brings
Fragrance on its downy wings.

The landscape brightens ! And the sun
His reign of glory hath begun,
And night's shades before him yield.
The ploughman drives his team a-field.
The tracks are soft and ripe the corn
Waving in the light of morn
Like plumes of gold ; sheep and kine
By hedgerows on the grass recline,
The soft and dallying Autumn breeze
Shakes the blossom-laden trees,
And in the sunbeam warm and brown
Bees are murmuring o'er the down
Bearing on their thighs the treasure
For their hive, and full of pleasure.
No lightning breaks, no rain-bow fair
Spans the spacious dome of air,
The peacocks and peahens no more
Gaze upon the sky's wide floor
In silent sorrow, but display
Their plumage to the lord of day.
Bounds o'er the lawn the nimble deer,
And birds are warbling sweet and clear.

Maidens ! Nature hath surpassed ye ;
No face can with the lotus vie,
No eyes so beauteous can be found
As the blue flowers that bloom around,
No brows though dark and bended well,
Can the ripplets' curves excel,
Nor can ye without shame compare
With creepers bright the vests ye wear.

Upon the margin of the lake,
Whose pellucid waters make
A mirror for the bending sky,
Herons and storks watch patiently ;
Young swans sail down all silver-white
Their feathers glancing in the light.
The round horizon's mingling blue
Is bluest now and charms the view ;
And rill and cloudlets, lake and sky,
Have each attractions for the eye.

Mark in the cool sequestered shade
Of yon wild and archèd glade
The damsel band ! fair they seem
Like bright spirits of a dream,
To deck their raven tresses, see
They pluck the full-blown *málati*.
Their looking-glass the lake serene,
Their couch the flower-enamelled green.

When all around seem bright and glad,
Why is the way-worn pilgrim sad ?
The wanton breeze, the flowering grove,
Remind him of his absent love ;
The mellowed moonshine for a while
Brought back her own bewitching smile ;
And now as shines the Autumn sun
On crimson flowers, the lips that won
His heart, when life a round of joys did seem
Appear as in a transient dream ;
And the dark eyes he loves so well
Cast o'er his soul a magic spell !

Canva's Hermitage.

(From the Sanscrit.)

It was a spot which Nature deigned to bless
With the cerulean hues of her own loveliness,
Sunfleckered vistas opening into glades
That gently lost themselves in denser shades,   .
Wild and luxuriant in their summer prime,
Laden with the rich treasures of the time.
Rocks tinted blue upreared their summits high
Afar, commingling with the bluer sky,
And bursting from its source upon those hills
Flowed broad and clear, Malini, queen of rills,
On its sloped bank was seen at dusk or dawn
The "bird of hundred dyes," the timid fawn,
Here opening flowers in colors bright arrayed
With *cusa* grass a varied carpet made,
And there the tendrils of the Madhavi
Half hid the old stem of a banian-tree,
Forming a fairy bower ! At the rain-falls
Safe housed therein the *chacravaca* calls.

On the east side the lowly hermitage
Of Canva stood, the venerable sage,
Constant in worship as well rites austere,
In all his speech and all his acts sincere,
He sought from fleshly bondage full release,
Dwelling apart, yet with the world at peace ;
Well versed in spells, his power the wood-nymphs
    owned,

Obeyed his mandates as of king enthroned.
Curling the smoke from sacred fires oft flew
While on the lawn the sun its hot rays threw,
And oft at morn or eve the groves among
The holy chant rose with the wild-bird's song,
Oft on the waters of the Malini
Were garlands gay and bilwa-leaves flung free
By pupils of the sage as offering,
As humble tribute to creation's King.

A single star is shining in the sky,
Its beams sport with the waves most lovingly,
And in that tender hour, that light serene,
Watering the plants three female forms are seen—
What are they? And is such rare beauty given—
Children of earth or *apsaris* of heaven?
Nymph-like they move and tend—the flowerets new
Receive the liquid life and weep adieu,
Peeping at those fair damsels as they go
Their raven tresses and their breasts of snow.

Now wakes to life the gentle southern breeze
Wafting rich odours from the sandal-trees,
And the *nagacessar's* fragrant dust is strewn
Upon each maiden's maiden-veil and zone,
And the round moon upon the water glows,
And lotus-chalices begin to close,
Each with due care plucks from the adjoining bower
For ornament a sweet *sirisha* flower,
And in loved converse all their thoughts engage
Slowly returning to the hermitage.

The Tomb of Sultan Baber.

(*From Indian History.*)

Not with a dirgelike moan
But with clear-ringing tone
Near Baber's tomb the sparkling river flows,
   Nor weeping willows wave
   Over the hero's grave,
But in a row the flushed pomegranate glows.

   Gaily at morning's prime
   Or close of bright day-time
On the gold fruits the golden sunshine falls,
   And in ' full-throated ease,'
   Now chiding, now to please,
To his loved mate the cooing cushat calls.

   There youths and damsels gay
   Keep blythesome holiday,
A trysting place for lovers and their vows,
   There tender words are breathed
   And wild-flower chaplets wreathed
To deck with their white shine fair maiden brows.

   His name inspires not fears
   As when with glittering spears
Ten thousand horsemen over India swept,
   Like whirlwind from the North,
   Riding in fury forth
And blood flowed free, and maids and matrons wept.

   But as in happier hour
   When lute and lay had power

And red wine flowed from goblets gem-enchased,
  And dancers all around
  Moved to the timbrel's sound
And jocund companies his rich tents graced,

  So under the blue sky,
  That glorious canopy,
Around his tomb his people love to sing,
  What time on earth and air.
  In rain-bow colors fair
Bursts the rich radiance of departing Spring.

  Flow, regal river, flow,
  And let no sound of woe
Disturb the spot where lies the conqueror proud,
  But let the wind and wave
  Sing love-songs to the brave
And from the groves a full choir chant aloud.

  Immortal love and joy !
  None may your power destroy
Though mortal bodies mingle with the dust,
  Though Time's Lethean stream
  Bedim the lance's gleam
And on the wall the warrior's sword is rust.

  And shower balm-dews ye stars !
  The trumpet-call of wars
Breaks not great Baber's trance serene and sweet,
  Let peace from the pure skies
  And heavenly harmonies
And earth's rejoicings still his spirit greet.

The Flight of Humaoon.

(From Indian History.)

At midnight'o'er the desert sands
   The monarch fled alone,
And in the light of paly stars
   His blood-stained armour shone.
Disbanded were his glorious ranks,
   His bravest chieftains slain,
Yet o'er his wide ancestral realm
   Once more he hoped to reign.

The gallant barb which he bestrode
   Had travelled far from home,
And his dun hide on either side
   Was wet with snow-white foam ;
But minding not his toil, he sped
   As swiftly as the wind,
To save from foes his regal lord,
   The kindest of the kind.

As horse and horseman onward passed
   Still feebler waxed the din,
The echoing tramp and deafening shout,
   And roar of culverin.
' Thou bear'st me well, my barb,' he said,
   ' Thou bear'st me well this night,
And I with jewelled bit and band
   Thy labours will requite.'

But ere another hour had passed,
   Down falls the noble steed ;

The king dismounts in fear and haste
   And looks at him with heed,—
Distended nostrils, starting eyes,
   And stiffening limbs display
That life with him is ebbing fast,
   And soon shall pass away.

Beyond the hills, by cloudlets ribbed,
   The broad-disked moon appears,
And o'er the vasty sea of sand
   Its crest of fire uprears ;
And far a-down the glimmering glen
   Advance with headlong haste
A hundred fugitives to seek
   The refuge of the waste.

And Tirdi Beg, the veteran chief,
   Among the troop was found,
The king accosted him by name,
   But looked he not around ;
He plied a-main his blood-stained spurs
   And passed his lord with speed,—
Thus e'er the cringing race behave
   When most their aid we need.

' Is it for this that from thy youth
   I reared thee in my hall,
And favours heaped on thee and thine
   From which ye feared no fall ?
Is this the guerdon of my love
   So equable and true ?

This night, ungrateful Tirdi Beg,
　This night thou'lt dearly rue.'

' Ho ! Tirdi Beg,' brave Koka cried,
　' Death light upon thy head,
Dost thou desert at utmost need
　Him at whose board thou'st fed ?
The flashing brand that's in my hand
　Shall cleave thy skull in twain,
If e'er upon the tented field
　I meet thee once again.

' My lord, my king, accept I pray
　A subject's proffered love,
Who, though despised at camp and court,
　Disloyal ne'er shall prove ;
The steed that bore my mother safe
　Is at my king's command,
And she upon a camel fleet
　Shall cross the sea of sand.

' The foe, the foe, I hear the drum,
　The trumpet's echoing peal,
I see the waving of their flags,
　The flashing of their steel.
A thousand dark plumes cloud the air,
　A thousand flambeaux burn ;
They speed, like eagles from their home,
　Among the mountain fern.

' The earth shakes 'neath their charger's tramp,
　Mount, mount my liege in haste,

Ere like the wild and fierce Simoom
　　They sweep across the waste,
Where Tatta's mountain lift to heaven
　　Their diadems of snow,
Once more to rear thy banner high,
　　Great king ! we now must go.'

The borrowed steed, with lightning speed,
　　Forth darts into the wind,
The camel fleet brave Koka leads,
　　And follows close behind ;
And many a hairbreadth 'scape they made,
　　And trying toil o'ercame,
Till Tatta's lordly mountain peaks
　　Burst forth in garbs of flame.

And when again, by heaven's decree,
　　He won his father's throne,
He bade the heralds to proclaim
　　The deeds by Koka done ;
Jewels and gold—his royal robe,
　　And lordly 'states he gave
To him who perilled his own life
　　His monarch's life to save.

Humaoon's Re-Entry.

(From Indian History.)

———— Not as he fled
Across the desert-sands, a fugitive,
The silent stars gleaming on bloody vest
And tiar, and beckoning horse and man
To mountain fastnesses and solitudes,
But once more ' the king ' in right royal style
He came, the city-gates stood decked with flowers
And open, welcoming the gay cortege ;
The streets were crowded with a motley throng,
Who soon made way to honor him again ;
Merrily the trumpets sounded, the house-tops
Crowded with lovely women, and children
In holiday attire, loud echoed back
The wild fanfare.   Many a gilded barge
Floating in sunset glories on the stream,
With rowers clad in purple chanting songs,
Dipped low salutes as the long oars were plied,
With flower-enwoven mane a milk-white steed
Bore the loved monarch, while his mounted guard,
Gallant and gay, whose swords were sheathed
No more to see the light, behind him came.
Huge elephants with towers upon their backs,
Camels with odorous loads, and rattling cars,
And cloth of gold, and pennons fluttering,
Made up the complement of that bright scene.
As he alighted one long shout arose,
' So the good triumph and the wicked fall.'

Then in the palace hall the feast was spread,
And plates of gold shone like so many suns
With blushing fruits and choicest viands crowned,
And goblets gleamed with daintiest Shiraz-wine.
Before the guests partook the monarch spoke,
It was a simple and unstudied speech,
' The stars that rule a being's destiny
May set to rise again, fifteen long years
Of exile past I come, you love me friends,
Nothing strange, because I feel I love *you !'*

The Death of Himu.

(From Indian History.)

In war array the elephants and mettled coursers stand,
The red sun gilds their trappings rare and lights the waste
of sand.
A thousand pennons laced with gold, like meteors wildly
play,
And evermore the trumpet-peal proclaims the coming fray.

The mounted soldiers in the van, the foot-guards in the rear,
On either flank the archers and many bristling spear,
And girt by twice two hundred blades is seen the blazing
car
Of him the leader of the host, amid the ranks afar.

His form is lithe, his stature tall, his bearing proud and
bold,
His turban is of twisted steel, his arms inwrought with
gold,
A girdle round his slender waist, a jewelled dirk he wears,
And in his hand, with grasp of power, a naked sword he
bears.

"Now sound the drums—they come—they come,—I hear a
mingled roar
As when the storm-fiend heaves the sea and waves dash on
the shore,
Unsheathe your sabres all at once, then rush into the fray,
And let the vaunting cowards rue the dawning of this day.

The dust-cloud screens the bannered files, I see their
    crescents gleam,
A long array of burnished shields flash back the morning's
    beam ;
Form columns, form ! in torrents pour upon the thirsty sod
The dread libation to appease your God, your father's God."

A hundred drums at once beat high, at once their swords
    they drew,
But wildly from the Moslems rose the well-known " Alla-hu,"
And cannons dealt destruction round, as with a loud acclaim
The hostile ranks in conflict met, mid smoke and din and
    flame.

The mounted troops of brave Himu in wildering terror fly,
For lo ! a hurtling shaft had pierced the gallant chieftain's
    eye,
Senseless and bleeding for a space he lies upon the ground,
Then mounts in haste a noble barb, and bids his trumpets
    sound.

He bids his trumpets sound once more, his standards shine
    on high,
Once more with voice of thunder shouts for death or victory,
Draws out the bloody dart and eye and hies with lightning
    speed
From rank to rank, his white plume shines where'er his
    troops recede.

The charging lines before the foe retreat in wild dismay,
And now they burst upon his flanks, his bravest bands give
    way,

And Kulli with three thousand horse has hemmed him in
    a ring,
" Chains for the traitor, ho" ! he cries, " who dares insult the
    king."

Bound hand and foot with chains of steel they led him from
    the field,
Gloom loured upon his manly brow, his grief no tear revealed ;
Bereft of dagger and of sword, his long locks stiff with gore,
Proudly he stood before the king with his red wounds all
    before.

Fierce Kulli, captain of the guards, spake out in accents loud,
" Now monarch, slay with thine own hand Himu, the bold
    and proud ;"
The king unsheathed his jewelled blade, and to the throng's
    surprise
He gently touched the captive's head, and tears burst from
    his eyes.

" Shame on thy ill-timed clemency," the captain-general said,
" Shame on the heart that shrinks to strike the false, false
    traitor dead,"
And e'er the king could stay his arm, or speak a single word,
He from the royal hand had wrenched that keen and flashing
    sword.

Right soon he dealt the deathful blow, the head was sundered
    sheer,
Then smiled a ghastly smile of joy and fixed it on his spear ;
And shouts for this most bloody deed resounded to the sky,
And many a piercing fife proclaimed the glorious victory.

Akbar's Dying Charge.

(*From Indian History.*)

This is no time to weep, my son,
   By weeping you do wrong,
But bear thee up right manfully,
   And in God's love be strong.

Lovely and large thy heritage,
   As lovely as a bride,
To keep her still thine own gird on
   That bright sword by thy side.

See now it hangs on yonder wall
   (For powerless is the hand
That wielded it in hunt or fray)
   My own, my noble brand.

Read what is writ on either side
   And write it in your breast,
Those characters of gold shine clear
   ' The merciful are blest.'

Upon the jewelled hilt or haft
   The diamond-sparks bespeak
The grasp around it must be pure
   Though not infirm or weak.

At honor's beck, in kingdom's cause,
　Like lightning let it fall ;
With power avenge the oppressed and wronged,
　And justly rule o'er all.

The blood-stains on the polished steel
　At mercy's fount make clean,
And may thy battle-fields right soon
　With waving crops be green.

In all the triumphs, all the joys
　Which thy good angel brings,
Forget not to give glory, son,
　To God the King of kings.

His blessing crave, his grace implore,
　Alike in weal and woe,
Long be thy reign in this fair land,—
　I go where all things go.

Noor Mahil.

(*From Indian History.*)

" O let me see my noble lord, and let me clasp once more
The hand that set this seal of death and kiss it o'er and o'er,
No fickle love is his, I know, that changeth with the day,
A love as strong as rooted rock that steadfast is alway ;
It cannot be that noble he should thus demand the life
Of one he wooed to be his own while yet another's wife,
'Tis false Mohabet with his wiles has forged the Emperor's
    name,
Is burning in his thirst for blood to do a deed of shame."

Thus spake she to the messenger as shone the morning sun
On the white canvas of the tents, her toilet-work was done,
Her charms a livelier flush had gained for tear-drop and for
    frown,
And over her dark tresses gleamed the topaz-circled crown.
A consciousness of being loved gives mastery over fears,
And she in this proud consciousness before her lord appears,
A flash of light, a radiant dream, he sees in wonderment
The peerless form of Noor Mahil in his imprisonment.

There sat Mohabet, valiant chief, whose own good sword had
    won
The fights which quelled the hosts of the Emperor's rebel
    son,
Too soon Jehangire's ire against his trusty servant rose,
For many slandered his fair name and many were his foes,

But he who threatened gyves and wrack himself a prisoner
    made
Was kept in noble luxury, was honored and obeyed,
Rich viands, music, jets and flowers within a palace grand,
The Rajput guards were all around, none braver in the land.

" Is it a crime my lord, my king, to love alas ! too well,
To wield the golden rod with power when from thy hand it
    fell,
Is it a crime my lord, my king, for thee to God to moan,
To wish to see thee once again upon thy father's throne,
Is it a crime my lord, my king, for woman's soul to rise
With the arrow deep infixt like an eagle to the skies ?
If these be crimes then nevermore thy love again I claim,
Then mine be all the punishment, for mine is all the blame.

But ah ! if duty urged me on, and nerved this feeble hand
To guide the war-horse in the fray or wield the flashing
    brand,
Then all I've thought and all I've done my lord will sure
    approve,
The headsman's stroke must need revoke and love with
    greater love,
The guards are peering all around as here I weeping stand,
A queen and yet a culprit for whate'er thou mayst command,
Speak but the word and fearless to the prison-cell I go,
What cares this wretched miscreant for me or for my woe ?"

Mohabet smiled, he knew her crimes, but yet he saw it plain
That he that signed the writ to slay, himself in truth was
    slain,

He waved his hand, the guards dispersed, and then he left the
    scene,
So beauty and valor triumphed, for she of both was queen :—
A lovelier form than Noor Mahil's ne'er sat on India's throne,
A prouder heart than Noor Mahil's in woman ne'er was
    known,
In palace-hall a shining light, in camp a flaming star,
All eyes were turned to Noor Mahil alike in peace and war.

Lodi.

(*From Indian History.*)

They galloped, mad-gallop, o'er field, through wood,
Their garments besmeared with their loved ones' blood,
It was night and the stars above were few,
Cloud-flakes hung dark while the moon struggled through,
The wind it sounded a sad requiem-swell,
To the loved and lost a mournful farewell,
The striped hyena in wonderment stood,
They galloped, mad-gallop, o'er field, through wood.

Behind them was heard the pursuers' cry,
The Chumbul before flung foam-froths on high,
The broad stream had swollen by months of rain,
It tossed, it groaned, like a Triton in pain,
On either side of the turreted bank
Like tresses dishevelled hung osiers dank,
And far in front, forms looming and strange,
Rose the mountain-heights of the Vindya range.

Near a rocky gorge over-grown with reeds
They halted and turned their swift-flying steeds,
They halted and turned, the gallant men three,
Lodi the brave and the sons of Lodi,
Their brows were most sad, their followers were few,
But faithful and tried and of mettle true,
All silently by that stern, silent rock,
They stood for the approaching army's shock.

Now in the east there are glimmerings of light,
The foe rushes on with their sabres bright,
They charge, but fall back, for the desp'rate men
Are hacking a hundred while they hack ten,
"Fly father," says Azmut, "'mid the wild jar
What boots it to fight this unequal war ?
Fly thou, save thy life, plunge into yon stream,
Leave *us* to die here as soldiers beseem."

With a tear in his eye, whirling his brand
Lodí clears at a bound the strip of land,
The stream bears up deftly rider and horse
(Though writhing and tossing in all its force),
Who with his ears pricked out and startling neigh,
His neck, crop, and mane, all white with the spray,
The opposite bank of the Chumbul gains,
And his master once more gives loose to the reins.

He quits his own Malwa's eastern confines
And is galloping o'er the diamond mines
Of Bundela far-famed, where temples fair
Lift golden cupolas into the air,
Stops there a while but soon leaves them behind
And gallops as gallops the moaning wind,
The good steed unflagging his master brings
To the tombs of Golconda's line of kings.

He was noble and brave, as hero should be,
Nor fawned on the great, true-hearted Lodí ;
Sternly defying the Emperor's wrath,
He brake his high plans and crossed his proud path,

Sorrows he conquered, great perils he past ;
And fell on the field of battle at last.
The whizzing hot ball through his target ran,
He fell and his guard was cut down to a man.

So ended the days of those sons of the free,
Lodí the brave and the men of Lodí.

The Taj.

(From Indian History.)

Where should beauty sleep but in a palace
Gem-enchased and vast ! Bring the wealth of Ind
And build me such an one and on its walls
Inscribe, in golden characters, the faith ;
Raise a white dome and lofty minarets
And steadfast let the crescent-pointed spire
Point up to heaven.   Form a large rotunda
Of marble, and enclose the central spot
With screen of trelliswork in marble whereon
May flowers of every hue perennial bloom,
Not those which bud, expand, and fade away,
But worked mosaic with gems and precious stones,
Cornelian, agate, lapis-lazuli,
And others that lie hid in mine or sea.
So construct the dome that voice of anger
Or unhallowed merriment shall call up
Loud chiding echoes from its sounding depths,
But whispered words of love shall be prolonged
Like far-heard anthems sung by angel-choirs.
All around, a garden in which cypresses
Should shade the walks and yet the ground be starred
With blossoms, and from blossom-spangled glades
The bulbul chant love-ditties to the rose.
And in that spacious garden, here and there,
Set crystal vases gleaming white and fed
By fountain jets, grove and bending sky

Glassing themselves in a pellucid tank.
Nor should be wanting other trees which yield
Refreshment to the weary traveller,—
The mango, citron, orange, plum, and peach,
Whose juices nectarine serve to allay
E'en fever-thirst and life and joy impart.
From age to age the palace and the grounds
Will form mementos of enduring love,
Such love as has been mine and now I feel,
Such love as Mejnoun to his Leili bore,
Or Khusroo to the beautiful Sheri,
Such love alone is registered in heaven.
Stranger! whoe'er thou art whose footsteps roam
Within the precincts of this monument
Be mindful of its sombre sanctity,
Nor with rude jest nor with unthinking laugh
Its silence break, nor with the spoiler's hand
Displace the gems, but pause and meditate
On heavenly love, and her who is in heaven.

Aurungzebe at his Father's bier.

(From Indian History.)

The monarch lay upon his bier,
    Censers were burning low,
As through the loft arches streamed
    The setting sun's red glow.
Still grasped he in his hand the blade
    Which well-fought fields had won,
And Aurungzebe beside him knelt,
    Usurper proud and son !

Remorse had stricken his false heart
    And quenched his wonted fire,
With gloomy brow and look intent
    He gazed upon his sire :
Can tyrant death make *him* afraid ?
    Hot tears burst from his eyes
As thus his grief found vent in words
    To the warrior-train's surprise.

"Father, thou wert the goodliest king
    That e'er the sceptre swayed,
How could I then lift up my arm
    Against thee undismayed,
How could I send thee here to pine
    Usurp the peacock-throne,*

---

* Constructed by Shah Jehan. It took its name from its resemblance
to a peacock with his tail spread.

O had I perished in the womb
   That deed were left undone.

See, all is changed that was estranged,
   Awake my sire, my king,
See, soldiers in their war array
   Thy son in fetters bring !
Thy rebel son who will abide
   Thy word whate'er it be,
And fearless meet the wrack or steel,
   Rise up once more and see !

Thou wilt not hear—thou wilt not speak,
   It is the last long sleep.—
And am I not a king myself?
   What means these stirrings deep ?
O foolish eyes, what means this rheum ?
   I will not call them tears ;
My heart that nothing e'er could daunt
   Is faint with boding fears.

The past appears ! a checkered field
   Of guilt and shame and war,
What evil influence ruled my birth,
   What swart malignant star ?
Why did I barter peace of mind
   For royal pomp and state ?
Mad for the baleful meteor's gleam,
   With worldly joys elate.

Remembered voices speak my name
    And call me parricide,
The murdered Dara beckons me—
    He was thy joy and pride :
And thus I fling the dear-bought crown,
    But whither can I fly ?
The awful thought still follows me
    That even kings will die" !

The Rakhi.*

Wear, wear this fillet round thy arm,
  Thou brave and noble knight,
Thy gallant war-horse paws the ground,
  Impatient for the fight.

A sister's love for thee hath wrought
  This silken tie so fair,
That thou protected by the gods
  The deadly fray may'st share.

Thy flashing eyes full plainly tell
  Thou'lt not disgrace the band,
If e'er the impetuous tide of war
  Roll where thy loved ones stand.

And sheath not, knight, thy gleaming blade,
  Till routed is the foe ;
And as the chaff before the wind,
  Before thy ranks they go.

And when by glorious Victory crowned
  Thou tread'st the bloody field,
Spare, by my tears, the wounded foe ;
  Be thou their help and shield.

But hark ! the tocsin's quivering peal
  Bursts on my ear from far—
Mount, mount thy steed that proudly neighs
  To join the ranks of war.

---

* Is a cincture of red silk or thread expressive of the closest ties of fraternal relationship.

Tarra Baee.*

(*From Indian History,*)

She sat upon her palfry white,
   That damsel fair and young,
And from the jewelled belt she wore,
   Her trusty rapier hung ;
And chieftains bold, and warriors proud,
Around her formed a gallant crowd.

A helmet clasped her forehead fair,
   A shield was by her side—
The helmet was of polished steel—
   The shield of bison's hide ;
And as she spake, the evening air
Disported with her raven hair.

' From girlhood, I have shunned the sports
   In which our sex delight,
And learnt instead to use the sword,
   And wield the falchion bright ;
To meet the tigress turned to bay,
And guide the war-horse in the fray.

' From girlhood, I have vowed a vow
   Our honour to redeem,
And make my noble father's name
   Of every song the theme ;

---

* The Star of Bednore, the heroic wife of Prithi Raj, the Troubadour of Mewar. A monumental altar, erected to their memory, is to be seen near the fortress of Komulmair, a fortress, I am told. singularly picturesque in appearance rising tier above tier mid chaotic masses of mountains co. vered with the *cactus* which luxuriate amid the rocks of the Aravulli.

To rescue Thoda from the slave
   Who lives to fill a coward's grave.

' And till my life-blood's purple flow
   Stands stagnant in my veins,
That early vow to see fulfilled
   I'll spare nor strength, nor pains—
To those who join me in the war
I'll be a radiant beacon star !

'My hand—'tis his who foremost scales
   The ramparts of the foe,
And to the wicked Lilla deals
   The dread avenging blow ;
Go, warriors—these alone decide
The man who wins me as his bride.'

The Capture of Torna.

(From Indian History.)

Through the keen March air its sounding way
   The blast of a horn is winging,
While there and here gleam shield and spear
   And bridle-bits are ringing.

In that mountain glen live gallant men
   Who own nor king nor law,
At their chieftain's nod they bend their bows
   And eke their swords they draw.

This morn in Torna's wooded vales
   The gathering-call sounds long,
And Torna beetles on the crag
   With towers and turrets strong.

The jocund sunbeams sportively
   Advancing, leaping fast,
Kindles on them light which seemeth
   A conflagration vast.

Those gallant men, but ten times ten,
   Resolved to do or die,
Have pledged to take ere close of day
   That fortress strong and high.

(Nor lacked they due encouragement,
   Their heaven-sent leader gave
To each a talisman of power,
   Thus braver waxed the brave.)

' Marked ye, ' said he, ' the fiery glow
   Around its white stone-towers

Y

The gods are ready to help us
 To-day the place is ours.

The gods are good, no human blood
 In this our raid shall flow,
One dash and cheer—all shall be clear,
 We soon shall find it so'.

In light and shade the band arrayed
 Thrice draw the tough bow-strings,
Three hundred arrows cloud the air
 And Torna's brass gate rings.

Then galloping with bristling spears
 They rush to gain the height,
A shout from the stern leader bursts
 ' See, see, again that light' !

And though on Torna's highest tower
 His purple flag is flying,
No blood its court with marble laid,
 Or outward slopes is dyeing.

The kilidar for his life now sued
 And owned the forest-lord
As victor, and at once laid down
 His turban and his sword.

Within the fortress' vaults were found
 Bright gold, and many a gem
Which served in coming time to grace
 Sivajee's diadem.

And Neera's flood that through the wood
 Ran singing, and each tree
Moved by the breeze, did celebrate
 This bloodless victory.

POEMS.--MISCELLANEOUS.

Glimpses.

When musing sadly on the days gone by
I sit all lonely at the hush of even,
To greet me then with every tearful sigh
Come unseen visitants from God's own heaven.

In sober silence doth my spirit hold
Converse with those impalpable to sight,
The true nobility, the tried, the bold,
The loved and loving, children of the light.

It is not fancy—for can fancy give
The holy calm that settles on my breast?
The world of turmoil in which here we live
Is not far distant from the world of rest.

The soul encased in this gross body's prison
Hath sympathies that largely will expand
Yes, all through the beamings of that Sun arisen ;
These are but glimpses of the heavenly land.

Nor are the lessons which those angels bring
Useless in balancing life's wild career,
Strong in each duty—meek in suffering,
To be what they have been—are whispered clear.

But there is one in that blest company
Whose silent language throws a deeper charm

O'er all my senses, and who seems to be
My special guardian set to save from harm.

" Say—radiant spirit—where is thy bright home?
And what in heaven thou lovest now to do ?
That flowing robe whiter than white sea-foam,
That crown with gems like sun-tipped drops of dew,

Whence are they thine ? for while thou wast here
The partner of my griefs, in humbleness
Thou spent'st thy days"—I heard that voice so dear
" Do thou the same and God will surely bless."

Roses.

Roses! Roses! Roses!
Falling as I stand
From the bowers of Eden,
From higeian land!

Roses in my garden
Shedding soft perfume,
Roses in my vases
In the blush of bloom.

Roses on thy dark locks
And thy garment's hem,
On thy breast a rose-bud
Just pluckt from its stem.

All around me roses,
Roses large and small,
Roses upon canvas
Hanging on the wall.

Roses on the carpet,
Roses on the screen,
Those are glowing proudly,
These 'mid leaves of green.

Prattling human roses
With their dew-lit eyes
Smiling, playing, hiding
For some gay surprise.

Ever thus may roses
Lighten my life's gloom,
And in radiant colors
Burst upon my tomb.

Lines.

Fair stream ! upon whose flower-enamelled side
   Listless at eve I love alone to lie,
   Whose placid bosom mirrors tree and sky,
I'll sing of thee—thou art the landscape's pride !
Now 'neath o'er-arching boughs thy waters glide,
   Now brightly laughing 'neath Apollo's eye,
   Wild and impatient as the winds blow high.
And more than calm when softly they subside.
Well hath the poet said O sparkling river,
' A thing of beauty is a joy for ever' !

Those Cinnamon Trees.

Those Cinnamon trees ! those Cinnamon trees,
Fondly I love those Cinnamon trees,
With their ovate leaves and silky flowers
Turning to fragrance the dripping showers
From every slender and bark-bound stem,
O how I love to muse under them !

Cassia or Balm of Gilead Fir
Can never my soul with such feelings stir
As when, while sinks the sun's broad zone,
I walk in the Cinnamon-grove alone ;
Thoughts lovely come with the rising breeze,
And I love the more those Cinnamon trees.

Once they belonged to that forest of gold
In which Sita, the peerless, sorrowed of old,
Transplanted with care o'er inland and sea
They graced the borders of famed Araby ;
In Yemen the happy, they sturdily grew,
Feet washed by sea-waves and tops by dew.

But ah ! I confess it is not for these
That I so love those Cinnamon trees
That at morning and noon and close of day
With them so often I speak and play,
Now guess, dear friend, what may it be,
That hath so endeared the trees to me.

One sultry noon with mind tempest-tost,
Thinking that all I had won was lost,
For solace, O Trees ! I came to you
Listened, and heard the ring-dove's coo,
Then all my doubts were put to shame
On the odorous bark I saw my name.

Those Cinnamon trees ! those Cinnamon trees !
Fondly I love those Cinnamon trees
With their ovate leaves and silky flowers
Turning to fragrance the dripping showers
From every slender and bark-bound stem,
O how I love to muse under them !

Night.

(*A mental picture.*)

O'er the brown and parchèd land
Night stretches forth her ebon wand,
Countless orbs their beams have lent
To light the azure firmament,
While with a steady ray from far
Brightly burns the polar star.

The crescent of Diana shines
Faintly through the hoary pines,
While the long shadows which they make,
Gleam dark athwart the placid lake,
Startling the elves that shun the day,
But nightly o'er the waters play.

And all is hushed—no other sound
Disturbs the stillness so profound,
Save what the green sea-billows make,
While bursting winds are all awake,
Sleep silent earth! while thus to thee
Old ocean sings her lullaby.

Ruins.

Is this the spot where monarchs proud
   Erst held their regal sway,
And suppliant courtiers thronged around
   Their biddings to obey ?
Are these the relics of the hall
   Where beauteous damsels sung,
Whose fretted roof and tapestried wall
   With peals of music rung ?

The portals from which issued once
   A hundred men abreast,
(With glittering spear and bended bow,
   And shield and waving crest)
With trees and wild shrubs over-grown
   In smoky ruins lie,
And view their image in the stream
   That murmurs plaintively.

The owlet from the rifted tower
   Sends forth a boding scream,
The bat now wings his heavy flight
   Beneath the moon's pale beam.
The raven rocks her callow young
   Upon her downy breast,
The spider in the dreary nook
   Weaves out her filmy nest.

Tho' years roll on, yet in their strength
   The rock-ribbed mountains stay,
And as it rolled at dawn of time
   So rolls the sea to-day.
But man and all his mighty works
   Are doomed to death alone,
Then wherefore lose the precious hours
   We yet may call our own ?

Sonnet.

INDIA.

O yes! I love thee with a boundless love
Land of my birth! and while I lisp thy name,
Burns in my soul 'an Ætna of pure flame'
Which none can quench—nor aught on earth remove.
Back from the shrouded past, as with a spell,
Thy days of glory memory recalls,
And castles rise, and towers, and flanking walls,
And soldiers live—for thee dear land who fell.
But as from dreams of bliss men wake to mourn
So mourn I when that vision is no more,
And in poor lays thy widowed fate deplore,
Thy trophies gone—thy beauteous laurels torn,
But Time shall yet be mocked;—though these decay
I see broad streaks of a still brighter day.

Sonnet.

An Indian Morning.

The clouds at night their darksome ranks advanced,
And rains descended in continuous floods
O'er my lone bower and o'er the encircling woods,
As through the air the fitful lightning glanced,
But genial sunshine gilds anew the sky,
The stately trees are bathed in golden light,
All nature laughs with transports of delight,
All nature joins in one glad symphony ;
At such an hour 'tis ecstacy to stand
On some green upland, and from thence to view
The far-off mountains mingling with the blue,
And all that God has lavished on the land,
To kneel upon the flower-besprinkled sod,
To kneel and lift our suppliant souls to God.

Sonnet.

GANGOUTRI.

'Mid frowning rocks with wild-shrubs overgrown
The river hath its passage found ; lo ! now
It comes, fierce foaming, as 'twould drown
At once all substances in its track.   Below
A bristly front the shattered crags present,
A bristly front the stunted trees display,
That meet with pride supreme the sheer descent
Of foaming waters ! The resplendent ray
Of morning gilds the sky, and as the breeze
Scatters in diamond-showers the living spray
Around the ruined stones and leafless trees,
A rainbow crowns the air ! A moment stay,
My friend, and mark, the torrent chafes along
Fretting and whitening as it sings its song.

A Sigh for Winter.

Oh, when will winter come again
    To bless my hearth and home,
That I once more on dew-decked lawns
    With buoyant steps may roam,
And drink the cool fresh morning air,
And bask beneath the sunlight fair ?

In northern climes the songs are few
    That sound hoar winter's praise,
Yet there for aye he loves to dwell,
    Mantled in silver haze ;
To us his passing visits seem
As fleeting as a pleasant dream.

The day-god from his throne on high
    Darts down his fiery beams,
And like a sheet of molten gold
    The lake's still water gleams ;
The foliage of the trees no more
Retain the glossy green they wore.

'Tis silence all, save when in gusts
    The burning blast sweeps by,
And like a voice denouncing woe,
    It sounds along the sky ;
Oh, when will Winter in his train
Bring back health-giving winds again?

No clouds defile the azure arch
   That spans the spacious earth,
The creatures of the fields no more
   Run races in their mirth.
All—all retire ;—the very snakes
Seek the cool shelter of the brakes.

Oh, when will winter come again
   To bless my hearth and home,
That I once more on dew-decked lawns
   With buoyant steps may roam,
And drink the cool fresh morning air,
And bask beneath the sunlight fair ?

Toil.

A LYRIC FOR THE AGE.

No nobler brotherhood can bind
Man to man or mind to mind
  Than the brotherhood of toil,
    None can ever
    That link sever—
  Up and work, sons of the soil!

Toil, the strong cement that ties
Zealous souls, comes from the skies,
  Ever conquering, ever sure,
    On sea and land
    Its trophies stand,
  And from age to age endure.

Poets, statesmen, heroes, sages
In all countries, of all ages,
  Lived anxious lives of toil and care :
    What generous fire
    Their names inspire,
  Their noble works are everywhere !

Stately ships at anchor ride
On the river's swelling tide,
  Like strong fortresses they stand :
    O'er seas they go,
    Though rough winds blow,
  And bring rich goods from every land.

Mark the iron-horse advancing
(While behind the smoke goes dancing),
  Moving with a thundering noise)
    So bouncing, strong,
    With train so long,
  Keep her right and tight, brave boys !

The message which upon its wings
From lands remote the lightning brings
  The needle's quivering tongue explains :
    The dark is clear,
    The distant near,
  We hear the clang on battle-plains.

Green spots of verdure meet the eye
Where sterile soil and brazen sky
  Repelled the sight with stubborn glare ;
    The trowels ring,
    On bare wastes spring
  Schools, hospitals, and buildings fair.

Then loudly let Toil's anvil sound
If Toil such blessings scatter round,
  And swiftly let his high wheels go :
    Though none can guess
    God's purposes,
  In patience let each toil below.

Fancy Pigeons.

Small wooden houses set in row,
    All painted white and green,
For fairies or for dapper elves ?
    Or some proud elfin-queen ?
A Lilliputian neighbourhood !
    Full of the sounds of life,
Of feasting, cooing, (ceaseless hum)
    And of vain-glorious strife.

Who are the denizens ? — I see ;
    Most fairy-like are they,
With mottled breasts and wings of blue,
    And necks so glossy-gay,
There's Lady Fantail, high-born dame,
    With Dragoons at the gate,
And Tumblers to mount up and vault
    Her queenly beck await.

One Trumpeter, a swarthy Moor,
    The lists is pacing proud,
Ran ta ra ra ran ta ro,
    He sounds his trumpet loud.
A Horseman with his spear in rest
    Darts at him in full speed,
Mark, how they grapple, tug, and strain,
    Mark, how the warriors bleed.

Bald-pates and Beards in council sit
    With Owls and Helmets, long,

To regulate the common-wealth,
    And judge of right and wrong.
Cases of tort (as lawyers say)
    Come up most rapidly,
Assaults, ejectments, and such-like,
    But none for bigamy.

Miss Barb with scarlet-circled eyes
    Is now so deeply in
With dandy Turbit and his frill,
    To hold back would be sin,
The Carrier to invite the priest
    Is flying from the bin,
But ah ! must all the truth be told
    About this Capuchin ?

Not far from his own home there lived
    A pensive pearl-eyed Nun,
A heart which many tried to win,
    But no one yet had won.
Last evening about sunset time
    I saw with mine own eyes
The old gray monk in sportive mood
    Fly with her to the skies.

The Two Flowers.

(From the French.)

Besides a garden's winding walk,
(When flowering-plants all knew to talk)
Two plants close to each other grew,
Fed by the morning's pearly dew.
Their names I shall at once disclose,
The Tulip gay and scented Rose.
But envy mars the happiness
Of those whom all men do caress.
" Are not my tints," the Tulip said,
" More bright, more various, than the staid
And queenly Rose's ! Why doth she share
More of the gard'ner's love and care ?"
The gardener Hodge did overhear,
And thus replied in accents clear,
" Dame Tulip, 'tis not for outward part
I love, but qualities of heart."

Moral.

External beauty charms the sense,
But never calls forth love intense :
Who in heart-qualities excel,
They bind us with a magic-spell.

The Two Asses.

(From the French.)

With panniers stocked and well supplied,
Two donkeys to the market hied ;
And to each other, as they went,
In praise of self their long ears lent.
Saith Master Grison to his brother,
" What fools be men thus us to bother,
As drudges, we come of noble race :
They yield not us our proper place.
The steeds they deck with trappings rare :
Can such with asses hold compare ?
In manners, courtesy, we excel,
In other qualities as well ;
And as to voice, O when we sing,
Do we not make the village ring ?
Is this not true, dear brother, say ?"
Aliboron did loudly bray !

MORAL.
Silly people fond of glory,
Like the asses in this story,
When they can find none other elves
To praise them, often praise themselves.

The Two Books.

(From the French.)

Two books each by the other stood
Upon a book-case of teak-wood,
One gilt and bound in green and gold,
The other was worm-eaten, old,
" I cannot," the gay volume brags,
" Bear amity to one in rags,
A finished gentleman like me
Should be in better company.
Where on this earth doth beau or belle
Side by side with the vulgar dwell ?
Away Old Book, thou'rt so unclean,
I like not friendship with the mean."

Next day to the bookseller's stall
A student came, glanced over all
The well-filled case, then as he pried,
The loving neighbours soon espied,
Took down the volume that was old,
Read, admired, and bought it with gold.
The other now engaged his mind
But nothing in it could he find
Worth reading, and the knowing elf
At once replaced it on the shelf,
Saying, "the binder all his pain
Hath spent upon this trash in vain."

Moral.

It is in quality of mind
That true nobility we find,
Your 'pink of fashion' oft may be
The very dreg of infamy.

APPENDIX.

The Lord our Righteousness.

Jer. XXIII—6.

My God, how perfect are thy ways !
    But mine polluted are ;
Sin twines itself about my praise,
    And slides into my prayer.

When I would speak what thou hast done
    To save me from my sin,
I cannot make thy mercies known
    But self-applause creeps in.

Divine desire, that holy flame
    Thy grace creates in me ;
Alas ! impatience is its name,
    When it returns to thee.

This heart a fountain of vile thoughts,
    How does it over-flow,
While self upon the surface floats,
    Still bubbling from below.

Let others in the gaudy dress
    Of fancied merit shine ;
The Lord shall be my righteousness,
    The Lord for ever mine.

                      COWPER.